The MATING HABITS *of* STAGS

The MATING
HABITS *of* STAGS

RAY ROBINSON

First published by Lightning Books in 2019
This paperback edition published in 2020
Imprint of EyeStorm Media
312 Uxbridge Road
Rickmansworth
Hertfordshire
WD3 8YL

www.lightning-books.com

ISBN: 9781785631382

Cover by Ifan Bates

British Library Cataloguing in Publication Data
A catalogue record for this book is available from the British Library.

Printed by CPI Group (UK) Ltd, Croydon CR0 4YY

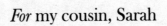

For my cousin, Sarah

HARDRAW FORCE,
1964

Jake and Edith followed the sheep-trods up the side of the fell, moving through last year's bracken frost-scorched a deep rust colour. They paused to catch their breaths, taking swigs from their water bottles, listening to the wheels of lapwing in the sky. Soon they made it up onto the rocky plateau. In the distance, the peaks of the Lake District. In the middle distance, the Howgill Fells, Garsdale and Sedbergh, the place where Edith grew up and lived until recently. Jake had asked about her family on the drive over—more out of courtesy than any real interest—and her breathing had gone quiet and she muttered a non-response.

Among the clints Jake pointed out mouse-ear hawkweed and bloody crane's-bill. The implausibility of such colour in that landscape of scree, granite, limestone. A wind was getting up with a brittle edge and so they headed to the cross-shaped shelter and sat on the wooden perch, staring out, summit after summit bathed in after-washes of light.

He took the flask from his knapsack and they shared some sweet hot tea, supping in silence. She tipped the dregs out and placed a hand in his.

She said, You still haven't told me why we're here.

I'll show you, he said, and went to stand up.

Let's just sit here a while.

The wind. The views. His hot pulse.

It's the highest point in Wensleydale, he said. Third highest mountain in the Dales.

You charmer.

Most southerly place you'll find yellow marsh saxifrage.

Eh?

Saxifraga hirculus. Reason I brought you.

Sexy-what?

Saxifraga.

I love it when you talk dirty, Jacob.

He squinted at her. It's rare.

Rare as a good man?

Flowering period's short. I thought—

A poetry to it he just couldn't express.

In an arch tone, she said, So this is your idea of romance? You been reading the Brontës or summat? Dragging a girl all the way up this blasted mountain to show her some flowers? Is this where you bring all your conquests?

Aye. And you're the first to complain.

The flutter of her long black eyelashes as she laughed.

He stands on the doorstep and whistles me out,
His hands in his pockets, his shirt hanging out...

She palpated and pinched the pad of his hand with her fingernails. He willed himself not to flinch. Presently the stone shelter felt weighted in silence, or perhaps a mood, an inner weather of hers he hadn't been

8

exposed to yet. What was it like in there today, Edith? Gales? Sleet and snow? Mist and fog patches?

Come on, she said. I need a drink.

She put her arm through his and dragged him back down the mountain, descending moorland the colour of rain.

The pub was quiet. After a couple of drinks, they exited the rear of the building and followed the path through the overgrown gorge to Hardraw Force. She was tipsy and kept touching him. The beck was in spate, the foss roaring around the amphitheatre, plunging a hundred feet in a single amber-coloured spout. He was about to speak when she turned to him, placed a hand between his legs and squeezed. He froze, eyes wide. Laughing, she ran towards the water's edge and began to undress. He'd never seen a woman completely naked before, something so wild and dangerous about her as she turned to look at him and grinned, and with a long-limbed, feline movement, she jumped in. She emerged on the other side, beside the swirl and mist at the base of the foss, waving at him to join her, her shouts and laughter swallowed by the clatter of water.

He thought he'd be like a lot of the old farmers he worked for, going to dances and trying to get partnered up but never having much luck, more used to looking at a cow's arse than a girl's, married to the first one that showed any real interest, a girl from the dale who knew exactly what kind of life she was letting herself in for, keeping house, raising a brood, helping out on the farm, unmithering. But Edith would have no real inkling of the hardness of his days or how much he loved returning to the softness of the nights in the cottage with her.

The sex at Hardraw Force that afternoon, and the months that followed, was white hot, feral, dragging him deeper into himself than he'd ever been. But looking back over those early years he could see it was more about making a baby than lust or passion. She wanted as much of his muck inside her as possible. But his muck was useless.

Once William was born, she just didn't see the point. He cuddled up to her so many times, impetrating for some physical love, but the wild older woman who skinny-dipped at the foss and fucked him so hard he thought his brains would tear loose, was just an echo in his skin.

Part ONE

DALBY FOREST

Jake reaches for his rifle, steps over to the glassless window, listens. A swap of wind scurries through the abandoned mill, a wind made of leaf mould and rusted rabbit wire. He realises where he is and what he is doing. Absolute dark around him. The plop and patter of rainwater, a liquid metronome. And with the sounds of the night swelling around him, he finds he can hardly breathe.

There: pine needles crunched underfoot.

He flicks on the torch. Something takes shape in the circle of light: pair of amber eyes, white blaze along the low-slung body. Badger tiptoeing into the night.

He flicks off the torch and steps out of the mill, following the sound of the badger among the thick bracken, crosiers furled and glossy, tilting his face up to a gap in the canopy, low burn of starlight. Something blissful about being deep within the forest, the shelter adequate and game plentiful, but the screech of an owl makes his heart pulse quicker. Then a stag roars, a deep *kronk* echoing through the trees.

Soon, in the next week or so, the first frosts will arrive. He has to be smart, parsing his next moves, because he'd rather die out in the weather than hand himself in. Prison cell? Freedom? The choice decides the kind of man you are. Not allowing himself to linger on what he'd done—*possibly* done. Wondering how many days he should leave it before heading to Noah's place a few miles north-west of here. Noah is Edith's kin. He always called her auntie but in truth she was a half-cousin.

Jake knew his age made him almost invisible but he also knew the police would be looking for an old man on a quad bike and so he covered the bike with branches and fern some distance from the mill.

Those first few days reconnoitring the forest, avoiding the scenic-drive roads and open picnic spaces, the mountain bike trails and walking paths of the forest's southern riggs.

Pre-dawn. The almost human moan of wind in the flue of the mill's tall chimney. Adjusting his trapper hat, he scratches at his scalp. Out in the trees the cries start again, a *yip-yip, yip-yip*. He blows warmth into his gloves. On the ground beside him, slugs ride the morning dew. He gets to his feet, stretching himself into the new day. He grabs his rifle and follows his route along the northerly edge of the forest.

From this overlook the only life he's seen over the past few days was a woman on a black steed, slapping its flank, oblivious to the old man watching.

Stalking the woodland around the boggy thwaite, checking the treetops for squirrels and birds, treading as quiet as he can, trying to blend in with the surroundings. Eyeing the game trails, a few bottlenecks beneath a fallen tree trunk, wondering should he set a few loop snares or will they just attract a Forest Ranger's attention?

The conifers give way to maple, ash, hazel.

Movement. Forty yards away: pink-footed geese. Six, seven of them.

But there is too much brash between Jake and the birds. He drops a leaf into the air to test the wind direction and stalks nearer. After a couple of minutes, he singles a bird out. Lifting the stock to his shoulder, he waits for a clear shot. Slips the trigger. Blood in the air, red mist suspended in a moment of death and beauty. The bird flaps for a few seconds and stops. He breaks cover. Clean headshot. Good size.

When the gun presented fire, the bird came tumbling down,
This lad he killed it with his club, before it reached the ground…

The day is starting to warm up a little. Nearer to the mill he hears squirrels barking and wonders should he play the waiting game, but after five minutes not a single one shows face. He gathers some chickweed and sorrel and Wood Ear mushrooms from the base of an elder tree.

As a younger man he was always on his knees in sidings and lanes, hunting for fruits and nuts and ceps. It used to tickle Edith, the way he'd pop plants and flowers in his gob, grinning at her. But she loved the flans he made from sweet chestnuts, and the pine needle tea and mallow wafers. But not as much as the sloe gin. Picking the berries after the first frosts so their skins were soft and juicy, shaking the jars to release the sugars. She liked taking the berries from the bottom and dipping them in chocolate.

He heads to the beck to gut the goose, dipping his hands into the chill water, reading the text of bird and animal prints in the mud.

Eight days eking out a blissful rhythm like this until one night he wakes to hear voices not far from the mill. Studying the teenagers through his rifle scope, three boys and a girl sitting around a camp fire, passing something between them, a canister of some sort and a plastic bag, sucking on it. Like twitchy animals. One of the boys turns and stares into the dark as if he can sense Jake watching. A light rain falls in the canopy above, a *plink-plink* on the tin roof. They'll come into the mill soon.

Time's up.

Astride the dirt-splattered quad bike, pulling through the subterranean-dark forest onto the moor, soon he comes to the dale where Noah lives. He hides the quad in a laithe among bird shit and sheep bones. Bending double to ease the weight of the backpack, he readjusts the straps and then trundles up the hill to study the keeper's lodge. Snagged on the fence wire next to him: creamy-white fleece fluttering in the wind, tufts of wool in scabs of blood.

Dawn breaks with the sound of antlers clashing on the moor—a lek of stags going at it.

Wisps of smoke rise from the chimney pot, churning straight and true. Old beat up Mercedes in the drive, car doors propped against a ramshackle lean-to at the side of the house. Scabby-looking donkey in the field scissoring its ears, flicking its tail. Above, skylarks chirrup in a blackberry sky. There it is again, a dull thump like a drumroll. He turns and spots a pair of ears, pink and lucent in the first yawn of day. A hare thumping out a warning to him, making him grin.

He heads down the field, passing through the low wooden gate into the garden gone to seed. Plastic containers. Water butt. Fence made from old doors. Small pond full of windfall. With his hands cupped around his eyes, he presses his face against the front window. Cobwebs. Husks of dead flies. He moves around the side of the house and finds the back door unlocked.

Noah?

Funk inside, something like wet dog and gone-off food. At first the silence swarms his ears but then he notices an insect-like ticking—grandfather clocks. Then something like a breath, a breeze through an opened window, the house alive to him.

Noah?

From the cluttered hallway he can see into the living room. Flock wallpaper. Spider-webbed lightbulbs. Dusty taxidermy on the walls. A guard around the fire. No sign of a woman or bairns around.

He heads outside and jimmies the lock on the nearest outbuilding and steps into the gloom. Workbenches. Electric saw. Tarpaulin. Propane cylinders. Cobwebbed seed trays. Pair of ladders hanging from the ceiling. At the far end, an old Nissan van. He tries the next outbuilding but it is secure. Behind him, the rattle of a chain and ballsy growl. Turning, he sees a mutt tied up in a small enclosure next to a dilapidated caravan.

Back in the kitchen, he leaves the back door open in case he needs to bolt, rests the rifle on the table and scans the room. Welsh dresser with vintage crockery. Hutch cabinet containing tins and jars. A creel on the ceiling, filthy towel hanging down. He opens the fridge, removes a Tupperware container, puts the stew in the microwave and sets it to two minutes. He opens a cold can of coke and drinks heavily. The microwave pings. He eats with hunger, leaning against the sink. Soon, he hears the rumble of an engine approaching. He grabs his rifle, glances at the open door. Watches Noah's clashy Land Rover coming down through the trees, thrum of tyres as it passes over the cattle grid. The lad's alone. He opens the front door, wipes his boots.

Jake calls out, Noah?

Ducking low under the doorframe, Noah enters, the pain of shyness in his face. They pump hands as if their lives depend on it.

Noah says, How long you been here?

Jake can tell by the hitch to his voice—he knows. Not long, he says.

Noah in his camouflage cargo trousers and puffa jacket like a territorial army nut. Jake says, Expecting any visitors?

Nope.

The police contacted you?

No.

Barrel-chested, enormous ears like mug handles, Noah removes his coat and hangs it on the back of a chair, retying his ponytail, hair the colour of chopped cedar and eyes an almost see-through blue—the same as Edith's.

Noah says, Been what, twenty years since I saw you last?

Later. The living room is cluttered, fire blazing, too warm for comfort, the grandfather clocks going off at different times.

Jake says, Doesn't that get on your tits?

What?

The gongs?

Don't even notice them any more.

Raised by his grandparents, Edith's first cousins, Noah's old Moors accent with just a slight and halting difference to the Dales.

Jake likes Noah because he never speaks about himself. No self-importance, no braggadocio. He knows he won't ask about Edith. Lad didn't even come to the funeral last year but they weren't that kind of family.

Jake waits for him to say summat.

He used to find it irritating the way the farmhands goosed Noah. He was big-bellied and jokey and everyone's friend and men took advantage. But his size could scare you, towering over you with his bulk like a sofa on legs. The way Edith used to fuss over the lad. Big daft lummox. Like a giant loaf of bread. Always smells of lard.

Finally, Noah says: It's true, then? TV. Pictures of you leaving the nursing home. Wanted in connection.

Connection?

Noah looks confounded, a hard quality to his gaze. Says, The old man's dead.

Jake nods.

Noah crushes his beer can in one hand and opens another. Furze of stubble, thicket of brows, eyes checking Jake over. The conversation moves on to oil and feed prices, as if Jake hadn't killed a man ten days ago and is now the focus of a manhunt. Jake's beer going warm in his hands. Noah emptying one can after the other. The stag's head on the wall observes them both with dusty eyes. Outside, the mutt barks a few times and then stops. Jake glances towards the window. The dread of things unseen.

Would you like me to run a bath? Noah says.

Jake nibbles his beard hairs, frowns.

Noah clears his throat. I'll get some bait made. You look fagged out.

As the bath fills, Jake props the rifle in the corner and strips, noting his unclean chest hair and fingernails. He lowers his limbs into the water and sets about giving his carcass a good scrub, scum on the surface of the water already. A falling-asleep breeze comes through the window. He sighs into the steam.

Charles Monroe, dead.

Sometimes you cross the line and there's no coming back.

He rinses himself with the plastic jug and climbs out to find there isn't a towel on the sneck and so he dries himself with his long johns. Rubbing a hole in the fogged-up mirror, staring at his reflection.

Night-time, listening to Noah's snores crank up in the next room, the occasional gongs and chimes of the grandfather clocks downstairs. Jake empties his backpack and sets the things out across the floor, examining each item in turn.

You've got to be smart.

Single-man tent in its compression sack. Pegs. Torch and batteries. Sleeping bag. Mini-camping stove and two gas canisters. Twine. Water bladder. Mess tin, knife, fork, spoon. Matches and a lighter. Solingen hunting knife. Co-op bags containing food, sundries. A box of 2:2 ammo. Snare wire.

The radiator click-clicks. Jake scans the room. Noah's grandmother still haunts the dreary space. Perfume bottles. A hairbrush spun with silver hair. Dresses in the door-less wardrobe.

He cracks open the window and lies in the near-dark scratching at the white bristle on his neck.

Two hours later something wakes him—an engine idling. He swings his legs from the bed and grabs the rifle, peeping through the curtains.

Slanting rain in the headlights of a 4x4, dark figure skulking from the outbuilding over to the vehicle.

Jake steps out of the bedroom to find Noah on the landing, raising a hand. The sound of the vehicle turning in the yard outside, moving through the gears, over the cattle grid and up the lane.

Noah reaches over, lowers the barrel of Jake's rifle and says, I rent him the old chicken shed. Comes and goes all hours. I don't pry.

I asked if anyone came.

Forgot.

You forgot.

A few hours later Jake is still clutching the rifle to his chest. There it is again—Noah's basso cough. Gongs of a clock. A jigsaw of early morning light falls through the window, otherworldly shadows in the room. Stretching his wiry limbs, Jake reaches into his pocket and removes the folded-up photograph of his son, William, and the postcard from his friend, Sheila.

He sniffs them, returns them to his pocket.

Down in the kitchen, he eats some ham and cheese and a pickled onion from the fridge. Listening to the house, assuming Noah has gone back to bed, a brief rain shower hits the panes.

After William's death, Jake tried to assemble all of the happy moments in his head. And the unhappy. And the mundane. As if this would help keep William alive in some way. Because the worst thing was the forgetting. Like when William stopped eating meat for a while. He'd ask to go to the loo during a meal and then hide the half-chewed flesh on the tiles behind the toilet rather than flushing it away. His queer but cute baby language: peel the balala, Daddy—look at pretty fowlers and flutterbies. He liked peeing on the dog and sleeping halfway up the stairs and drinking puddle water. Jake would lift him from his cot just to bathe in his sleepy smell, kiss his minuscule feet and fingernails and eyelashes.

Making a snowman in the garth, a misshapen thing with broken twigs for teeth and rotten quinces for eyes. Jake asked him what they should call it. Without hesitation: Let's call it Edith.

Edith often complained she never really had any time to herself. She always seemed desperate for some headspace. Some mothers wanted to know everything their kids were doing at all times, what their homework was, who they liked or didn't like at school, but Edith just wanted to talk about other stuff and have a part of her life that wasn't just about scraping shit and goo off things.

But the memories felt so day to day, like obsessions that wouldn't leave him alone, becoming mono-pitched in his head. But maybe that was the point. Maybe it made them more bearable because nostalgia can become an illness.

Something snags Jake's attention: sounds from the living room—crackling, spitting. He finds Noah in the chair beside the open fire watching TV with the sound muted.

Thought you were still in bed, Jake says.

Made some bait for you. Left it beside the front door.

Right.

Not sure how you're set for clothes and what-not, but there's Pop's old stuff hanging in the cloakroom. Wax jacket, boots and gloves and that. Be turning cold soon. Help yourself.

Jake nods, thinking about scent dogs, tracker dogs. Wearing another man's scent.

They share a long look.

You've been busy, Jake says.

I'm only…You know.

Is the reason I trust you because I know you, or that I don't really know you?

Noah cracks a smile. Here. He passes Jake a wad of notes.

Jake nods. That's very decent of you.

No need.

Hate to ask, but there are a few other bits I could do with.

Noah folds his arms. Shoot.

Could do with swapping my torch with yours? The high-powered one. Some bin-bags. Salt. Gaffa tape. Garlic.

Course.

And the Nissan in the shed. How's it run?

Just replaced the timing belt. Starts first time.

It stolen?

No.

Owt else I should know?

No lights on the dash.

Throw in the Buddy heater and propane cylinder?

Noah cracks a smile.

Jake says. The quad. It's in the laithe near yon fork on the moor. He tosses Noah the keys. Keep it.

They spend the rest of the morning winterising the Nissan van, removing the back seats and insulating the floor with foam and bits of ply, using bubble wrap to seal the windows and vents, hanging fleece sheeting along the walls for extra warmth.

Why don't you just head south?

None of your concern. Because I've never been here.

Who are you?

Got any whiskey?

Drambuie. Can't abide the stuff. Take it.

Jake runs his fingers through his hair. Got some scissors?

Five months earlier

SHEILA'S PLACE

She was waiting to greet him in the doorway. They embraced quickly, tightly. Howay in, she said, and led Jake into the front room where he took his haversack from his shoulder, pulling out a bottle of wine and a small jade plant in a terracotta pot. She positioned the plant on the windowsill.

It's from a cutting, he said.

Isn't propagation amazing?

Like putting a fingernail in soil and growing a whole new person.

She held his gaze, grinned.

They sat at the table and she dished out the food—salmon fillets, mashed potato, broccoli, asparagus. Robust and ruddy-cheeked, she was wearing a bonny yellow dress, low-cut, snug, her hair sleek and straight as wind-flattened grass. She was easy to smile, her eyes crinkling at the corners with laughter lines. Jake was in his tired-looking suit, four-day salt and pepper beard, iron-grey hair slicked back.

They had known each other in passing for years, just a nod and a quick now then, but since Edith passed they had begun to spend more time together in the Ox and he had come to rely on her company probably more than he should. Of course, tongues had been wagging. Not that anyone would say owt to his face. She was a lot younger than him—had recently turned fifty—and was well known around town. Blowsy, mouth on her. Jake liked her crass laughing talk though he had never heard her curse. He saw something noble in her, honest. The way she dealt with her daughter, Karen—useless lump of a lass, druggy, town bike. Sheila might as well be raising the grandkid on her own.

Jake said, It's not how far you fall, it's the way you land.

She raised a brow. Here was a woman who didn't appreciate being gainsaid.

She said, Karen and her boyfriend, they're talking about getting wed. Don't get me started. I mean, has he even got a job?

Could be the making of them.

Worst mistake she'll ever make more like.

He shrugged.

What? she asked.

He licked his lips. Nowt.

Rubbing the stem of her wine glass up and down, her eyes on him, he finished the last of his salmon and placed his knife and fork together precisely. She refilled his glass, emptying the bottle, collected the plates and headed through to the kitchen.

Staring at his reflection in the windowpane, at the gathering darkness beyond, he got an uncanny sense he was being watched by some unseen presence outside, his reflection doubled and vague—becoming his own ghost.

Just you, apeth.

She reappeared with another bottle of wine and said, I planned to get some cheesecake but Clem was going ape in the Co-op and it totally slipped my mind. She barked a laugh and retook her seat. Did you used to cook?

For Edith, she meant.

When he didn't respond she reached over and rubbed some dust from the windowsill. Then she started to tell him about her first husband, Steve.

Always coming home kaylied. Being shouty. Wetting the bed.

Didn't you and him want bairns?

I did. But he couldn't... You know. Infertile. For the best, looking back.

Did she see the heat in Jake's eyes?

With a half-smile, she added, He buggered off down to Leeds with another woman. I met Bear soon after and fell preggers more or less straight away. Started the whole sorry malarkey over again. Joking. Bear's a decent bloke.

Bear, her ex—a thickset biker who made a living driving a sidecar hearse, basically a covered coffin attached to a motorbike, a popular send-off for local gangs.

Jake cleared his throat. Seems the steady sort.

Scratching the curve of her neck, raising a red mark, she reached over and took a tube of hand cream from beside a plant pot and squeezed a drop into her palm.

She said, Did I tell you I worked on a farm when I was young? Remember the Pick Your Own on Hawes Road?

Course. Edith used to tatty pick there.

Always fancied a small holding, bit of land. Veg and chickens.

A nod.

Don't get me wrong, she said. I love care work. Know we get treated like crap and the pay is rubbish but care work is a privilege. The strength to give, strength to help. Can't imagine doing owt else.

Looking at him with her eyes dimming, it was as if she was tuned into his airwaves. I'm trying my best not to pity you—this was the kind of look she tried and failed, not to give.

Jake said, It's nice of you to spend time with me.

You're easy to spend time with.

Been hard. Don't mind admitting.

She reached over and placed a hand on his. She was always touching him, squeezing his muscles. Seventy-three years old but he still had the physique of a seasoned farmhand—tall, capable, strong. She pulled her hand away.

You're doing well, she said.

What way?

You were always someone I wanted to get to know better.

Why?

Because you seemed like a nice man.

Not doing this out of pity?

No.

Because you feel sorry for me? Think I'm lonely?

She said, We're muckers, aren't we? Well then. Good. Ignore what folk in town think.

Because I am, he muttered.

She bit one of her finger nails and spat it to one side, wiping her finger on her dress.

I'm always here for you, she said. You know that?

She reached across the table again and squeezed his hand.

His eyes wandered her face, neck, cleavage.

He said, Think we should call it a night.

JAKE'S PLACE

Dim lamplight, stale shadows. It was chilly in the bedroom and his pyjama top was unbuttoned, exposing a scribble of white chest hair. Rain plinked the guttering and sill, flicking the curtain so. Nights like these when a load of weather moseyed around the uplands, thunder soughing through the hills, leaving a stillness and smell of earth behind.

He felt Edith still existed somewhere, whether in his dreams or awake he was certain she was still trying to offer herself to him. He knew she'd gone and would never return, but she was hanging on, lingering—*somewhere*. Still trying to communicate. Still trying to finish the conversation that was their shared life. Or maybe the conversation they never had. Whatever it was, he never wanted the connection to end.

He straightened Edith's dress out next to him and then glanced towards the window. The solitary yellow light of Ted's farmhouse on the opposite side of the dale. Distantly a dog barked. Then another. Ted walking the cows, getting them ready for milking, collies nipping at their ankles.

Jake sings softly:

When she kenned she kenned in 'er beats,
Ti mak a print she put in 'er feeat...

Recalling his early days on the farms, the camaraderie of the young hands. Usually they kipped in a byre or outhouse together, singing and laughing and drinking into the night, making up songs about the working conditions and tight-fisted bosses or singing the old Yorkshire traditionals. The morning stillness of the parlours, the click and whirr of the machines, the heady mix of cream and iodine and shit in the air. Nowt better than seeing the cows lined up in their own stalls with their names on the wall.

She made a cheese an' put it on t'shelf,
She never tonned cheese while cheese tonned self.

Something about the memory makes his muscles tauten, his limbs knotted and stretched by years of manual labour. Mechanic, shepherd, foreman, hedge-layer, flint-knapper, lured from one farm to another to shear, milk, pluck, dress, slaughter—owt to addle some brass.

Oftentimes he stood by the window waiting for Ted's light to come on, wondering if Ted looked across the dale and saw the silhouette of Jake watching. A kind of company.

He stroked Edith's dress and then sniffed his fingers, eyeing the bedside table. The Western novel with its musty smell. Glass of water. The framed black and white taken not long after they first started courting. He stared at the image recalling their first date, the hike up Great Shunner Fell, skinny-dipping at the foss, losing his virginity.

Gradually the first light hit the clouds capping the horizon, lighting them obliquely from beneath, orange and then violet. Another sleepless night waiting for the dawn, listening to the excited chatter of the house martins in the nests beneath the eaves—nests that look like papier-mâché cups.

Eyeing the photograph on his bedside table again, he couldn't help but think about her end-days. She was always so quick-witted and fiery-tongued but then her mind began to slip. Like the day she asked where her mam was.

Jake, unsure, said, She passed away, flower. Long time ago.

Oh, she said—an inhaled and startled: *oh*.

A few days later he found her at the window.

Jacob, when did we move here?

He touched her arm. I'll mash us a brew.

But as Edith made her soft but rapid way towards death, it felt more like a disentanglement—addled from life, from reality.

He lay a while longer as dawn entered the room.

June meant the flowering of white cotton-grass and purple moor-grass. It meant the hatching of the lapwing and the blooming of damson blossom. The month drawing curlews back to the reservoirs and tarns to pair up, filling the moor with their bubbly skrikes—he always found it such a lonesome sound.

A noise beyond the bedroom door: there she was on the landing with her heavy-heeled steps, making her way downstairs. The creak of the second riser.

Edith neither dead nor alive but both dead and alive.

Running his fingers over her dress, sliding his nails into the crimped folds at the waist, he realized he hadn't seen her for over a week. Guilt pricked his conscience. It wasn't because he'd gone to Sheila's place last night, was it? Surely, she wouldn't begrudge him a bit of company?

He knew he had to face his loneliness head-on. Knew he shouldn't let it drag him further down or it'd get the better of him. He knew this. As long as he could ride his quad bike down into town and do a bit of shopping and have a quiet drink at the Ox, he'd need no help, no pity. Because amid all of this swirling sorrow he'd begun the difficult task of putting his life back in order. He just didn't know what it should look like without her in it.

Blue, wet light spreading in the east, a breeze purling through the window, bringing with it the scent of macrantha blossom. A bluebottle tapping along the ceiling, jangling his nerves.

He took the jar of cinnamon hand lotion from the bedside table and unscrewed the lid. Debossed in the cream: the contours of Edith's fingerprints preserved in time.

Present day

SCARBOROUGH

The cause of death has not yet been confirmed to us...

Sheila was at work when Bear texted to see if she'd heard. They say it's Jake. Feeling so heart-sore, confused. Scared, even. Can't be. Even if he was capable it just didn't make sense. Jake had never mentioned Charles Monroe before. Not once. What did the two men mean to each other? Must be some kind of mistake.

But then why has he disappeared?

Jake Eisner, 73, is accused of killing 78-year-old Charles Monroe during an incident at Wappentake Nursing Home...

The local police came to see her last week. Said she'll need to go back to Nettlebed to make a statement. She is certain they are watching her flat. Then there's what Bear said about Lip Monroe, Charles' son. Hunting Jake with a team of men. Lip wanting to hurt Jake.

The Monroes. Everyone knows them in the dale. They run the local shoots and beats and hunts. Charles was famous for shooting croquet balls from canons in front of his house. The family have lived in the bubble of their walled estate on the far side of the moor for a few generations, Charles' great-grandfather an émigré from somewhere or other. They made their money in the mills down in West Yorkshire and shipping in Tyne and Wear, but Charles' uncle gambled most of their money away and they had to sell the main mansion house. You see them in Nettlebed on rare occasions, poncing around in their Barbour and Hunter gear, flat caps and knee breeches and ridiculously expensive wellies. The townsfolk just think they're dozy rich twats who speak so posh they might as well be southern or Scottish the amount of sense they make—but that doesn't mean anyone wants them dead.

Detective Inspector Paul Kettlewell urged social media users not to speculate about the 'highly emotive' death...

Often, she finds herself at her living room window watching the street below, half-expecting to see Jake outside. The view of the North Sea and north-eastern skies often scares her. Gulls hovering on updrafts outside her window, their cries like children in pain. The dirty, salty weather, blustery other-world. The constant soundtrack of waves. Sometimes the sea looks unmoving like something lingering in shadow or fused with night, or made of cloud, hardly there. Not the romantic notion she had before moving to the coast, picturing herself wild swimming every morning or going out on the boat of some ruddy-faced fisherman who resembled Jake in a sou'wester.

The Chief Constable of North Yorkshire Police promised a 'full and thorough' investigation. He urged patience during the inquiry...

She stopped texting and phoning Jake a while ago because it was obvious he was rubbish at keeping in touch. She was expecting to see him at Christmas. Drinks and a singalong in the Ox. Cook him a meal. Have a right good laugh. Howay, come visit. Little holiday. Do you good. Maybe another slow-dance.

And I cannot let you in.

Into what? His heart? His secrets?

Is that why Jake didn't answer the door those times she called? Was he already unravelling? The rifle in the corner of the room. Hatching a plot.

Why didn't he just shoot Charles? There's just something so... intimate about it. Your hands around someone's neck, eye to eye.

A post-mortem examination gave the preliminary cause of death...

I know him. He'll be out there in the wilds. Or shacked up with some old farmer he used to work with. They'll never catch him. But I still don't believe he did it.

Thoughts like these.

Her phone is buzzing in her pocket. It's Bear. She removes her glove, swipes the screen. He asks her how her day is doing and then the conversation turns to Jake.

She says, Guess you've not heard owt?

A false lead yesterday. Police helicopter over the dale. They know he's armed. But the TV cameras have gone.

For the first two weeks it was lighting rigs and microphones and trucks with satellite dishes. The townsfolk have become wary of strangers.

Sheila takes the phone from her ear and changes hands. A seagull caws outside the window—a sound she has grown to despise.

Call me, she says. If you hear owt.

Later. She walks the full length of North Bay, searching for flotsam in the chill. She used to think of storms as cleansing and purifying but all around her are dead birds and scraps of fishing nets, shell grit and fish egg cases that pop underfoot. She places a small chunk of driftwood and a few shells into her shoulder bag and continues north until she reaches Old Scalby Mill where she sits in the bay window drinking coffee, watching a small boat taking tourists along the coast searching for dolphins and whales.

Her days are shaped by care work and grocery shopping and long meditative walks along the beach, and when she isn't working you will find her in the Merchant sipping a soda and lime. Owt but sit at home fretting about Jake.

She is walking to work the following morning when she gets a phone call from the police in Nettlebed. It takes her a while to make sense of what the officer is telling her.

We need to talk to you formally, he says.

After her shift finishes, she wanders down through the rain-dark streets to the empty foreshore. With the wind chucking her hair around her shoulders, she holds onto the cold white railings and stares out to sea. Fast food wrappers rattle in the flowerbed beside her, the sea wall slimy with diesel-stained wrack, raindrops knuckling at her skin, chilling her neck.

She doesn't want to go back to Nettlebed because of this. Owt but this. Her manager has agreed to give her time off but that isn't the point.

Where are you, Jake?

The interview room is stifling hot. Exposed brickwork. Clicking water pipes. A tiny window and a wall-mounted camera in the corner. The young police officer sets his files down on the table, takes a seat and starts clicking his pen. Sheila knows him. He was in the same year as Karen at school.

We need to establish what Jake's state of mind was when you saw him last.

Last time I saw him was back in mid-August. Went up to the cottage to see if he was all right. Think he was ignoring me. Can be like that at times. Wanting to be left alone, you know. Awkward.

He was being difficult?

Look, he's still mourning Edith. But he still has his marbles. More than me.

What's the nature of your relationship?

Eh?

36

If you don't mind me asking?

We're pals. End of. Unless you're of the persuasion a man and woman can't be just friends? But if you mean do I love him, then aye, I do. Like you do any close friend.

He casts a glance at the wall clock, writes something in his pocketbook and says, Did you know Charles Monroe?

Do I sound like I mix in those circles?

OK. Is there any family of Jake's—distant relatives, I mean? Old friends? Anyone he mentioned?

They're all dead as far as I'm aware.

If Jake decides to contact you—

I know.

As she climbs into Bear's car her composure collapses, a ragged fit of tears. It's as if all meaning has been drained from her life because deep down she knows Jake did it, that he is more than capable of killing another man. Bear places a hand on her shoulder, waiting for her to settle.

Dove Cottage. Between the tangles of potatoes and sprouts capped with frost, she eyes the house, recalling Jake in a very physical sense, and he is present to her right now and she fully expects to see his face appear at the kitchen window.

This time yesterday she was making her client a sandwich and cup of tea in his too-warm flat in the Old Town in Scarborough, and now, twenty-four hours on, she is scouring Wensleydale in vain for an old man who, she knows in her heart, has gone.

The light is clinging on.

She recalls a conversation with him, one of those rare moments when he opened up to her. Is it selfish, he said, that I wanted to die before Edith? How his eyes were trying to invoke something. Is it selfish when couples do that?

Sheila didn't know how to respond.

Howay, she says to Bear. Let's go.

Potter's Row. She steps into the stifling hallway, shouts, It's only me, Mam.

Mam in her chair. The room smells bitter.

Oh, so what do we owe the pleasure now that her Highness has deigned to visit?

One of Mam's favourite routines: playing the martyr.

Sheila leans down and kisses Mam's bristly cheek.

They sit in their usual positions, staring at the too-loud TV as if nowt has happened in the time since Sheila left.

Mam says, You sure Jake's not shacked up with you in Scarborough?

Is that what folk think?

What did the cops have to say?

They're worried about his state of mind.

No shit, Sherlock.

I mean they want to know if he was right when—

When what? When he choked Charles Monroe to bastard death?

We don't know that.

Mam sucks her lips over her gums. Always knew he was a bit touched.

Thanks for your support.

I've been looking at sheltered living in Scarborough.

Ha bloody ha.

You going to see your youngest daughter before you leave or have you forgotten what she looks like?

I'm off there now. You coming?

Nope.

Karen sitting maudlin in the living room. Sheila's flowers lie ignored on the side.

Where's Mike?

Out.

What's with the face?

I just don't know how any mother can do that.

What, Sheila says, with you being so experienced at motherhood and all? Who looked after Clem for the first six months while you gallivanted around town? Eh? Me. That's who.

Think there's summat wrong with you.

Aye, and it's hereditary.

Nana's been a right tit-ache since you left. Really pecking my swede.

Welcome to my world.

Won't have shag-all to do with Clem.

Mam does plenty for you and don't you forget it. And I don't just mean the hand-outs either. Yes, I know all about them, missy.

Karen laughs without mirth. A laugh that says fuck-you. She reaches for her fags. Sheila picks up the flowers and takes them through to the kitchen but she can't find a vase and so she uses a pint glass. She goes back in and puts the flowers right next to the TV—Karen's main focus in life.

The heavy hang of time in the room.

Sheila points at Karen's cigarette. Shouldn't you do that outside?

Whatever.

Think about Clem.

It's all I ever think about.

Where is he?

Fast asleep for once, so don't be going in and waking the little shit or I'll swing for you. And by the way—

What?

Jake.

What about him?

You know what.

It's got sod all to do with me.

You hiding him?

Don't talk daft.

I bet you think he's innocent, don't you?

I don't know what to think.

Well don't you ever slag off my choice of boyfriends again.

He isn't—

You know Dad still wears his wedding ring?

Sheila squinches her eyes at her. Well, I just wanted to see you. See you're OK. Let you know I'm doing fine. And my heart's OK, thanks for asking.

Karen, snidely: Everyone's talking about you.

I'll be at your dad's over Christmas. You're more than welcome to join us.

I'm coming whether you like it or not.

Good.

Oh, piss off.

Jake looks abashed in the image. Taken on her mobile at the Ox over the summer, he looks like he's had a few. That reluctant smile. That habit he has of licking his lips and scratching his jaw while staring into your eyes as if he hasn't a clue what you're on about. He hates having his picture taken. Recalling the lumpy sound of his voice. The way she would pretend to stumble into him, immerse herself within his strength. The way he held her in his arms and sang to her. The older the fiddle the sweeter the tune.

And I cannot let you in.

But you are in.

A knock at the door. She sits up, smooths her hair.

Come in.

Bear steps into the room. There's a fire, he says.

Dove Cottage was like a beacon over the dale that night. The sound of sirens bringing townsfolk out of their warm homes. The flames on the hilltop, tableau of fire fighters and police officers, Sheila at the moor-edge squeezing Bear's hand, the bounce and fall of dread inside her. Was Jake in there? Quills of snow were falling into the flames except it wasn't snow it was ash, smoke forming patterns inside, human shapes. Recalling floorboards creaking beneath his boots, the dim-lit rooms, his bedroom walls painted a murky green and brown, colour of a bad hangover, the patchwork quilt and the stains on the carpet, his hair in the plugholes and fingerprints on a whiskey glass and on the mirrors and windowpanes. The chronicle of touch. And that photo of them on the sideboard, Jake handsome in his suit and cloth cap, and Edith wasn't just pretty, she was stunning.

Gone.

She heard a noise and turned: thick-tailed fox with something in its jaws trotting into the dark.

She says, Jake?

Some nights she stands on her doorstep in Scarborough inhaling the night air, listening to the ceaseless rhythm of the waves crashing on the beach, a rhythm mirroring the wheel of thoughts in her head, because even in Jake's absence, even with all this distance, even though she knows he has gone, she can still feel his presence at the very core of her world.

HARFA HOUSE

Pulled awake by the sound of an engine outside the van. The slam of a car door. Jake's brain ever vigilant—it's exhausting. On his knees peeking through the side of the bubble wrap, he scratches a hole through the frost on the inside, botanical etchings on the glass.

A people carrier. A man with two small dogs. The man shouts something and the dogs run onto the beach yapping.

These stone-silent nights in the chilly Nissan van, shivering between the fleece-lined walls, the chill air puckering his lungs. The car park is situated just outside Marske-by-the-Sea. Behind him, arable land surrounds the village. Ahead, the dawn beach and coffee-coloured North Sea. He has been sleeping in the van for over two weeks, travelling up and down the coast road between Redcar and Flamborough Head, skirting Scarborough because he knows they'll have questioned Sheila and will be watching her place.

This past couple of nights he's been helping himself to veg from the allotment on the outskirts of the village—leeks, sprouting broccoli, Brussels, kale.

He cracks the window open—the sound of waves, wind, gulls skurling about. He heaves a cough into the crook of his arm. He is convinced the gas from the portable Buddy heater is toxic, wrecking his lungs. This queasy headachy feeling all day. Last night he decided: tomorrow I'll head back down to Harfa House. The remote farm where he used to shepherd. He needs to spend a night out of the van.

Another coughing jag, stooping him. It takes him a long time to catch his wind. He pulls on his trapper hat and gloves and emerges from the van confused, exhausted, slowly reassembling himself. The cold rives around him. But a lifetime on the land, inured to bad weather—he's as tough as a fell dog and barely registers it any more.

With his binoculars, he glasses the beach and dunes and farmland 360 degrees, as if he can read the landscape and secure some understanding from it. Just visible down the coast are Warsett Hill and the ochre cliffs of Saltburn. Seeing them again, he travels back to 1971, to that winter afternoon when Edith told him she was pregnant...

She said it without inflexion, all matter of fact, and every muscle within his body began to tauten. He shook her arm from his and stepped away. Kittiwakes fluttered around him on the glass-like sand, his face a dark knot as he weighed up the sky—it looked heavier than the earth.

He glanced at her sideways. This was the moment to walk away, draw a line, challenge her. But feeling such injury inside all he wanted to do is apologise and nowt about that made any sense.

We've been trying for so long, Jake.

She hated mawkishness and he had never seen her cry before. Her tear-wet face appeared pinkly translucent and then she dissolved before his eyes. He reached out, thinking she had disappeared, but then she moved into him, threading fingers. He kissed her cheek as her voice frayed on the wind: Well I'm pleased, even if you're not.

The crackle of her ice-blue eyes.

She stepped out of her shoes and walked towards to the tide-line.

He said, What you doing?

She glanced over her shoulder at him. It was the same look she gave him six years ago at Hardraw Force, the first time he saw her naked. She hoiked up her skirt and stepped into the waves, manes of sea-surf in the wild black sea, the scene burnished to a winter's greyscale apart from her pastel blue suit, the hem of her skirt darkening. Something so uncouth about it, as was the trill of her laughter, filling the emptiness between them, making him hum inside. Because he was always scared of what she would do next. Because he was scared she would be forever running into the sea and he would be forever watching her run.

That moment already taking on the hue of memory.

Later, driving back to the cottage that ached, she placed her hand on his thigh and told him she loved him. He didn't know whether this was an apology or an admission. Something ending, drifting. Something about to begin: another man's shadow kicking at his heel for the next forty-six years.

He took his hand off the steering wheel. Touched her long, cold fingers.

The engine stumbles, putters. The gauge says the tank is almost empty. He turns the radio off. A few days ago, he caught the tail end of the news: *The hunt continues for Jacob Eisner*... A sickening worm in his head.

He drives to the small petrol station outside Sandsend, a remote place that sells sandwiches and hot drinks and has a disabled toilet where he strips and cleans himself and washes his smalls. The solitary security camera points southward and so he always drives in from the north.

He fills the tank. As usual the place is deserted. Across the gravel lot puddles of oil reflects the neon sign beneath a clarty sky.

The owners are gobby, simple folk.

How do? the man says as Jake enters the warm store.

Jake nods. The wife is nowhere to be seen.

Jake takes a basket from beside the door, filling it with food and drink and a pair of sunglasses from the carousel. He knows better than to glance at the newspapers. Neither the man nor the wife has mentioned the manhunt but he knows it's out there. Over a month now. Or has the world lost interest?

The man is a mouth-breather, lips open, spittle-wet.

Ready for Christmas tomorrow? the man says.

Jake nods, pulling two twenty-pound notes from his wallet.

At the daughter's in Redcar, Jake says, inventing stories easier than he thought.

Very nice, the man says, and continues chelping while Jake eyes the parentheses of lines around his mouth—like he's spent his life grimacing at his ugly wife. Then Jake notices the burls of warts along his knuckles, like pale blooms, and realises the man is wearing his wife's cardigan, appliquéd pink and red flowers along the neckline. The man sees Jake looking and shoots him a glance—hot beads.

Merry Christmas, Jake says, and the man mutters, Same to you.

Snow-dusted moorland, flakes drifting the empty B-roads, dark cloudbanks gathering in the distance as he guns the salty surface of the road, drystone walls blurring at the edge of his vision. Slow down. He rubs his eyes. The same argument about the man in the petrol station has been running through his head all afternoon. Did he chat too long? Say too much? He takes his foot off the accelerator and opens the window. Trying to remember every detail of Harfa House, just one of the shuffle of North Riding farms he worked on over the years. Would anyone from the old days still be there? The owner, Warwick, was twenty years Jake's senior. Most likely dead. Warwick's son was such a fat bairn, like something moulded from marshmallow. What was his name? Running through the upland breeds they used to keep. Bluefaced Leicesters. Teeswaters. Devon & Cornwall Longwools. Older ewes drafted from

46

the hills, mated with the longwools to produce mule lambs, selling them to the lowlands to cross with sire breeds.

Passing through a deserted hamlet of stone cottages, so many tumbledown barns and abandoned farmhouses on this side of the county. Appraising them, making note, fully expecting to have to sleep in one some night. Presently he is out on the top of the world, the creamy draw of light so different up here, sparkling above the horizon, dark rind of escarpment, outcrop, smir of cloud, snow scalloped in the lee of drystone walls.

Turning off the main road, he follows the single-track lane for another couple of miles. Something unreal about this journey back in time.

Daylight beginning its turndown, first glister of starlight. Glassing the farmhouse knit tightly with black slate, broken panes, dimness, no vehicles, no sign of life. A gabble-rack further down the ghyll: geese on a pond of black water and ice. Two minutes later he is pulling into the driveway, slowing to a crawl, one finger on the steering wheel. Engine puttering through his thighs, he scans the windows and the cattle shed, woodwork flaked and blistered, rotted in places, hinges all rust.

He forces entry through the kitchen window. Sink and sides and table piled with mould-black dishes, food packaging and empty bottles. Cupboards bare. Squish of bird shit underfoot.

Anyone?

Rooms empty apart from the large pieces of furniture and a rotten three-piece suite. His staggered breaths, footfalls, the house eerily hollow, lonesome. A man's greasy handprint on the mirror, broad-leafed, air fetid with damp, tang of urine. Warwick is still here in a way and Jake fully expects to see him on his wooden settle beside the fire, hands outstretched towards the flames, or stuffing plugs of tobacco into his clay pipe—when he wasn't pointing the stem at you and remonstrating, that is.

Memories, for some reason, tinctured with regret.

He heads out to the van to get his backpack. The surrounding land is dark, quiet. Returning to the kitchen he finds a bucket and then gathers water from the beck in the nearby ghyll. He lights the fire, the room heating up nicely, then he boils some water and tips it into the sink and finds his bar of soap. Undressing, he eyes himself in the de-silvered mirror above the fireplace. Running the soapy water over his body, muscles flexing. He's thinking about the day Edith died, removing her nightie, squeezing the sponge, laying her out—her nakedness the only thing that felt real to him at that moment. He ties his boots, buttons his shirt, tucking it into his jeans and then pulls on his woollen jumper and combs his hair. Examining himself in the mirror, straightening his collar. Stares. Not a single face muscle moves. Recalling Charles' tongue hanging from his mouth like the labellum of some appalling orchid. He turns and peers out of the kitchen window, gibbous moon bathing the landscape silver.

One of the panes is broken and night seeps into the room. The old wooden bed with its stained mattress, scuffs on the walls like a tide mark. Fully clothed in his sleeping bag, the photo of William next to his head. Dusty hearth, wind soughing the chimney breast, the intimate smell of soot. He falls asleep with waves of expression breaking over his face but wakes with a gasp and turns on the torch. Reaches for the picture of William, staring at it for a long time. William's face glaring back at him accusingly. He climbs out of bed and crumps down the stairs into the kitchen and opens the back door. Glorious stench of sodden earth. Harfa House—he can't believe he's back here. But Charles is in the field outside, floating among the darkness, eyeing Jake with that rapt, arrogant look of the dying. Jake wishes he'd finished the job properly, choked the shadow from that bastard and seen the final flicker of life in his eyes, face flat as a gravestone.

Mid-morning, trudging down the snow-filled dale to the cascades. Ice-edged wind, gloss white shimmer of snow. To the south-west, the Sour

Milk Hills. To the east, the heights of Snilesworth Moor. The unchanged signature of the landscape returning to him. Gathering the flock of half-wild sheep from the fell, big gang of men bringing them down to the pens, shouts and whistles filling the dawn.

Ah feeds the pigs and milks the coos as happy as can be,
Then off ah gans ti ploo, me lads, and me heart's sae gay and free.

Soon he comes to the foss where he spotted the birds yesterday. He watches the water shimmering down the rocks, thinking about his younger days rabbiting with his old man: the pissy ferrets in a box, the yappy terrier, the .410 rifle and corpses twitching in his hands. How his boyish heart thrilled at finding the hare's smeuse. Father letting him set the snare for the first time. It felt like he'd always had a weapon in his hands.

Movement. He removes his gloves, lifts the rifle, feels the perfect weld of his jaw against the stock. Large greylag in his sights, finger covering the trigger—a crisp let-off. He lowers the rifle, squinting into the hushle of wind.

Come, all you gallant poaching lads, and gang along with me,
And let's away to Sledmere Woods some game there for to see.

It's Christmas Day, he realises. He feels such a comedown. All he wants is to return to Wensleydale. One more night at Dove Cottage. Sense her again.

My earnest wish whatee'er be my lot
Is to end my days here at home.

He eats the heart and kidneys as he smoke-dries the meat. Then he takes the lamp outside and opens the van, staring into the dark interior, forgetting what he has come out here for.

Fuck.

Headlights coming down the track.

Turning his back, covering the lamp with his arms, he can't find the off switch. Waiting with the liquid sound of blood in his ears, counting time. The engine noise grows louder, louder still. Then the vehicle comes to a halt outside the farmhouse, engine ticking over. Or is he just imagining it? Then moving through the gears westward up the hill.

Driving in circles throughout the night. It was probably just a tourist or somebody lost. Neighbouring farmer, maybe, seeing the light and thinking nowt of it. Almost dawn, he convinces himself he's safe and decides to drive back to the farmhouse, his eyes beginning to fade, head resuming its dreamy nod. Just before seven am, about three miles from Harfa House, he is reaching to turn the heater down when he hears a loud thud against the van. His feet shamble the pedals. The vehicle jolts, stalls.

He opens the car door. Just the red glow of his taillights.

He undoes the seatbelt and steps out. There she is at the side of the road, running an invisible path in the air. He nudges the ewe with his boot. Swaledale gimmer. The night remains so silent. He heads back to the van to check the damage. Just a dent. Returning with his hunting knife, he makes a deep cut at the angle of her jaw, drags her from the ditch and lets her drain a while.

Back at the farmhouse he attaches the carcass to a hook on the kitchen beam and loosens the skin on her hind legs before separating it at the hock. Then he yanks the hide down to the rectum, hooks a finger inside and pulls out a few inches of pipework, tying it off with twine.

He steps back. Folds his arms. Examines her.

Recalling bringing the gelds down from the fells to be smitted and jabbed. The endless fixing of fences to stop the buggers getting out. Shooting corvids at the end of the season, the sight of them banqueting on lambs' ket unpardonable. Castrating the crossbreeds, knife in one hand, nuts in the other. The Tan Hill shows, presenting the tups, preening, teeth checking, wool parting, lug inspecting. Usually not winning or getting any bids but there was always the epic piss ups afterwards.

Noo awd Dicky Thompson 'e 'ad a grey mare,
'E teeak 'er away ti Sedgefield Fair,
'E browt 'er back, Oh, yis 'e did
Becoss 'e 'adn't a farthin' bid.

The muddy, bloody chaos of lambing time, the ewe leaning over her dead lamb and yet the fell is full of them lowping about. You watch her watching them and can't help but feel for her. She lowers her head, licking at the carcass, the scent of her making and all that she is, and the moment always breaks your heart, not knowing how much she understands but knowing the pain must be marrow-deep. You lift the dead lamb into the bag and she follows you to the net and parracks. Then you skin the carcass and make summat like a waistcoat, holes for legs. You collect an orphaned lamb from the quad—a spare—and dress it up in the dead lamb's skin. Then lift it into the parracks and introduce them both. Hello. That's right. She sniffs its arse, licking at this stranger wearing her skin. And yes, it's nudging her underline. Yes, it finds the teat. It's in for the suckling. The ewe stands erect, closing her eyelids.

Love. It was all one continuous thing.

Rubbing his hands on his jumper, he steps towards the ewe again and opens her up, black guts crashing onto the kitchen floor. He'll leave her to hang for a couple of days before quartering her. He chucks the tripe, melts and lites into a bag for the days ahead and then fries the kidneys, eating standing up in the kitchen, daylight breaking outside.

New Year's Eve, mid-afternoon, listen to him snore, a deep and dreamless nap, fully dressed, his belly aching after gorging himself on meat. He wakes. A noise. He shuffles, poor footing over to the window:

a woman outside with a collie on a lead peering into the house. Then she edges around the back and out of view. He creeps across the landing and catches her curling a glove to the van window. She glances around. Meddlesome eyes. He tiptoes back into the bedroom and watches her trudge up the lane, lifting her phone to her ear. Time's up.

Nowt in his rear-view. Not the red neon jewel of the petrol station. No hint, even, of the dividing line between land and sky. Then something shimmers in the distance: New Year's Eve fireworks across Teesside. He opens the window, a wind full of moisture shunting through the van. He rubs his ears. You're fine. But the fleece sheets luffing in the back of the van are Edith pinning out the washing on a blustery day. *Going to give me a hand or just stand there watching?* Up and over the narrow moor-roads of Black Hambleton, snowflakes slicking the windscreen, he eyes the speedometer wondering about the pressure in the tyres.

He sees a sign, tamps the brakes, pulls into the car park. He climbs out of the van, breathing the night air. Tilting his head back—Ursa Major circles Polaris upside-down.

Hood pulled up against the wind, he clasps his hands together— Edith rubbing her thumb against his palm.

Soon, he reaches the northerly edge of the Moors, landscape melting below into the eerie orange fuzz of Teesside, Middlesbrough in night-bloom, the enormous black nothing falling ever so slow into the orange. But then the fluting call of a curlew is the factory bell rudely taking him back to that Friday afternoon, the end-of-shift bell, a two-syllable chime triggering the sullen exchange of workers in overalls, and here's Edith at the factory gates, the prettiest woman he'd ever seen. He was a rabbit frozen in hawk-shadow. He winked at her and she called him a cheeky bugger and he experienced such an explosion of happiness inside.

And here is a wanted man standing on the edge of Black Hambleton, on the edge of a new year. No idea what to do. Where to go.

Five months earlier

THE OX

Same again, Jake?

He was in his usual spot in the former smoking snug, a wooden curved affair decorated with old lamps and framed black and whites of the dale two fathers ago. The nearest photo showed townsfolk ice-skating on the beck. Jake liked to pretend he was one of the children in the image, skating arabesques. The barman brought Jake's ale through and removed the empty glass. Jake stared down at the brown liquid, turning the pint slowly on the beer mat. After a couple of minutes, the snug door opened and there she was.

Sheila: You right for a drink?

He nodded, beamed. She disappeared into the bar and he could hear her laughing. A minute later she came back through and sat beside him, sipping her vodka and coke. As per he asked how her mam was getting on and she gave him the same dispassionate rundown. Jake had known

Sheila's mam all of his life, a spirited sparrow with a shock of dyed red hair. Once a looker she was now a spry, potty-mouthed old bat.

A song started playing on the jukebox. Sheila began to sway, jostling him.

Howay, she said. Let's have a boogie. She got to her feet, extending a hand.

Don't talk daft.

She stepped away, moving her hips. Watching her shake and roll, under the ceiling light she looked pretty. Jake let his eyes wander her body for a moment. Something in his stomach churned. Jake averted his gaze until the song came to an end. Sheila plonked herself down next to him, breathing hard.

Jake shook his head.

On the edge of laughter, she said, What?

Later. Clamour through in the bar area and the lamps came on as Sheila entered with their fifth round and placed a whiskey chaser next to his ale.

Jake tutted. I shouldn't.

Because whiskey makes you frisky?

They're on my tab?

Oh shush.

I'm not letting no woman pay for my drink.

Dinosaur.

He lifted the glass to his neb, sniffed the peat.

Up your bum, she said.

It's to be savoured.

Ahw get it down your neck, man.

Guess it might help wash it down.

Wash what down?

Jake drained the whiskey in one long sentence. Nowt.

Then he saw her—Edith. She was standing beside the door, arms folded, a look on her face. It was like she was really there. So real.

Disturbing. But when he blinked she had gone.

He searched Sheila for some sort of reaction.

This was the first time he'd seen Edith in public, not just at home in his private moments. Drunk, fearful of seeing her again, it felt like everything was slipping away. Scanning the snug, expecting her to reappear, Sheila chelping on. Then the burning returned, a scorch to his lower abdomen.

Just spend a penny, he said.

Regulars acknowledged him as he lumbered by. The Gents was empty. Leaning against the wall above a urinal, he struggled with the front of his trousers and realised he was going to lose control. He staggered towards the cubicle, twining his legs. They buckled and with a look of surprise he stumbled, landing with a jolt on his knees. Crouching there for what seemed like the longest time, shaking, something drifted down from the ceiling: a skelter of leaves.

It was happening again.

He was back in the Outwoods, entering that dire memory, that twilit evening when he was twenty-four, watching Charles Monroe, a local toff—handsome, greased-up ginger quiff, moss-chop sideburns—enter the derelict woodsman's dwelling. Edith was inside, dressed for a night out, bouffant hair and pastel blue suit. Jake had followed her there, his suspicions proving him right. Picturing her inside, skirt pulled up among the leaves.

A hook in his gut forever leading back to that moment.

The high road out of Nettlebed became a single-track lane lined with hawthorn hedge and a run-off ditch full of clouds of frogspawn. At the end of the lane, before the cattle grid that led out onto Jackdaw Moor, where his plot of land backed onto the toast-coloured tapestry of tussock and peat, stood Dove Cottage, Jake's home for just over 50 years.

In the kitchen, the ding of the microwave brought him back into the present. He was in his dressing gown, hair damp and slicked, sitting in the chair next to the hearth, flagstones chilly beneath his feet. The farmhouse-style kitchen was a state of dust, chaos, half-eaten meals.

The washing machine banged in the utility room.

He rubbed his left arm, left leg. He'd feel it tomorrow. Sheila took the mug of soup from the microwave and passed it to him.

Peering up at her, he said, You've done enough now, lass.

She placed her hands on her hips and breathed a sigh. It was the first time she'd been to the cottage and he knew exactly what she was about to say.

I've made a start on those dishes, but flaming hell. You need someone in here.

He stared down into the mug.

She said, You're not coping are you.

It wasn't a question.

He turned to look at a framed photograph on the mantelpiece. The Kodachrome hues of an early Polaroid. His son, William, standing beside the beck cradling a rainbow trout in his hands, beaming into the camera, apple-cheeked, freckle-splattered.

Following his gaze, she said, Who's that?

He said, My sweet lad. And it struck him: how he never spoke about William any more. Never invoked his name every day just to make himself feel right. Though the weight of what would have been William's birthday tomorrow had grown ever more crushing over the years.

Jake, a man who wore his sorrow on the inside and rarely let it out, indicated the photo, pointing a finger. His voice failed. He tried again.

I'm a coward.

Misinterpreting him, she said, Shush. It's my fault for getting you so kaylied.

She touched his shoulder, gave it a squeeze.

There she was: Edith, a young woman again, standing behind Sheila, laughing soundlessly.

Sheila glanced around. What is it?

He got to his feet. Need to be on my own, he said.

The following morning, poised between the cemetery gates, a bouquet of daisies in his hand, he peered up at the church clock as it neared noon. Remembering how they used to make their way out into the morning light, to the florists to buy the same bouquet they did every year: seventeen daisies for each year they were blessed with him. Laying the flowers against the stone, Edith talking to William as if he was down there listening. Holding her hand but unable to reach her through all these years. Eyeing the distant sycamore where Charles Monroe had stood.

The church bell tolled noon. He turned and headed back the way he came. At the edge of the park he exited the kissing gates and began the climb, pausing near the top of the hill to peer across the dale. Witch's hat of the church spire. Corrugated roofs of cattle sheds. Black snake of the beck winding through the hills. It began to drizzle, blow. Swaledales made plaintive noises in the field beside him, curls of red smits on their arses. Up the overgrown holloway he climbed, following the clashy track along the escarpment, engrossed suddenly by the flickering acres around him.

The ramshackle building, an old woodsman's dwelling, four sagging right angles of mossed-over stone, tumble of masonry and fern beneath a stand of tall sycamores. Grass and moss in the gutters. Laburnum, cyclamen. Nature assimilating Jake's memories, regrets.

Standing on the threshold peering in. Remnants of dirty curtains hanging at the windows, a few of the panes still intact. In front of the fireplace the flensed bones of some long-dead stag.

He walked through the decayed squalor of the rooms, the gloom inside. Bird corpses. The gossamer of spider's webs catching the light. In what was the old bedroom he paused beside the remains of a bedstead and dropped the flowers down, as you would into an open grave. Wiping his neb on his sleeve, he peered to one side suddenly, as if expecting to find her here.

Forty-six today.

He waited.

I know you can hear me.

He moved over to the window, peered through a broken pane.

I'd been alone since the day he passed. But we were alone together. We had each other, didn't we?

He rubbed his face. Scratch of bristle.

I always loved him. And it didn't matter to me because you were so content. Even though you always knew I knew.

As he uttered the last word, a hunter's shotgun discharged in the nearby woodland, two flat retorts, making him jump. The manic *cok-cok-cok* of a pheasant.

He returned to Dove Cottage to find Sheila on the garden path, a couple of shopping bags at her feet.

He frowned. How long you been here? Curter than intended.

I know you're a private man, Jake. But let us make a start on that kitchen, eh? Get a proper meal inside you. She smiled more confidently. I make a mean shepherd's pie.

He opened his mouth as if to say a flat no, but then he scanned the moor, the sky. A storm was gathering. He'd hate for her to get caught in it.

He met her eye. Yesterday, he said.

She shook her head. It's nowt. Forgotten.

He smiled. Yes. It is. Door's open.

She picked up the carrier bags and moved inside.

He paused in the doorway, reached into his pocket. Edith's jar of cinnamon hand cream. Placed it on the low-set lintel.

Trying to change himself over the years. Trying to let go and be a better man. But deep inside all he ever felt was guilt and shame and fury. Because once you taste what's under the rage the hunger never leaves your mouth.

He stepped into the cottage, slamming the door behind him.

Present day

OLD TOWN

Following Sheila after her night shift down through the dawn streets of Scarborough, a salvo of fishy sea-wind makes Jake stagger, pause. Between a gap in the Georgian townhouses on Burr Bank, the view reveals the crab-orange rooftops of the Old Town, the lighthouse on Vincent's Pier and swatch of beach beneath the distant dark headland. In a garth to his left, a bright yellow stab in the gloom: hazel catkins hanging from a tree. And here's the joyful noise of a robin: *tea-cher, tea-cher*. It's as if his life has been lived in black and white this past couple of months and suddenly everything flips into Technicolor.

He continues following her, taking a left down Sandgate, past the pretty old church that houses the sea cadets where she stops to peer through the steamy window of a café.

It gladdens his heart to see her again. Doing so well.

Recalling meeting her in town one day last summer, her grandson in the pram. Picturing her returning home to the hum of his shit-filled nappy, hefting the lummox onto her hip and changing him on the kitchen table while her useless daughter watched TV and smoked weed.

Sheila, he says into the wind.

She appears to have forgotten something, turns right and heads back up into the gloom of the winding streets. He waits a minute and then makes his way along the Foreshore, up to the secluded side street on the far edge of Ramshill where he has parked the van.

That night, standing on the cliff edge, he watches nautical lights move slow out at sea. The sea below is oil-like, tarnishing the reflection of the moon, slick as the guilty thoughts in his head.

You there, flower?

Watching Sheila's flat on Eastborough the next day, waiting for her to appear and then trailing her up to the castle and down along North Bay, past the multi-coloured beach chalets and the Sea Life Sanctuary, between a huddle of schoolchildren in high-vis jackets. It appears she likes to beachcomb on her days off, searching for tide-dumped flotsam in the chill.

When masts and spars and broken yards
Came floating to the shore...

At one point she peers in his direction. He raises a hand but all she must see is an old man in sunglasses, parka, hat. She looks straight through him. All around are scraps of fishing nets, shell grit and fish-egg cases. He watches her place a few items in her shoulder bag and then examine the waves.

He looks around. No one.

Sheila, he says.

She doesn't hear.

Louder: Sheila!

She turns. He takes a few steps towards her, removing his hat.

Sheila, he says again, and she throws him a look, her eyes ablaze but numb.

No, she says, and turns and rushes away.

Later that evening he rings her doorbell and when she opens the door and sees him she drags him in and strikes him in the chest. He starts coughing, a real jag. Cursing, she pushes him into the living room. He moves over to the window to put some space between them. The smell of her in the room.

Get away from there, she says, and whips the curtains shut. With a huff she collapses into a chair, crossing her legs at the ankles, tugging at her bra strap.

He undoes the zip on his parka halfway.

Don't you be getting comfortable, she says, her expression falling just short of hostile. I see you now. For what you are.

And what's that?

If someone said to me a friend of yours is going to choke another man to death. A man who is sick, dying. Then just disappear off the face of the earth, only to turn up on your doorstep two months later. If they said how would you react, do you know what I'd say?

No.

Neither do I. Because I'd think they were mad. It's terrible, Jake. I can't—

Her lips gather into a knot. He wants to cross the room and hold her. He is only five, six steps away but there is a force field surrounding her, some benevolent force. She stares down at her hands as if expecting to find residue on her fingers, as if his presence has dirtied her.

She says, If you're not going to talk to me then you should leave.

He turns left, right. His eyes bounce off every surface, every object in the room. On the sideboard, the lime green numerals on her clock flash zeros, as if his presence has broken time.

Why'd you do it? When he doesn't respond, she adds, He was dying.

For a long time.

What does that mean?

He feels dizzy. He takes the smallest of steps towards her, entering her force field, and coughs into his fist.

She says, Takes some doing, choking someone to death. Looking him in the eye. That's commitment.

Her gaze makes the air vibrate. Her mouth looks stiff. There's something numb and distant inside her he just can't reach, some dark kernel of let-down, of disappointment. He wants her to challenge him, to articulate the unsayable, undeniable.

Hand yourself in. Let me call them.

Don't.

With sarcasm she says, Or what? Her expression heats the room, bending everything they mean to each other.

He coughs again, spluttering into cupped hands.

He notices the jade plant sitting in the window. Stares at it.

She says, How long you been in Scarborough?

Few days.

They've been watching this place.

I know.

Not just the police.

Who?

Other men.

When?

Couple of weeks.

You know them?

Bear does, aye.

I need your help.

I should call them right now. Where you sleeping?

Got a vehicle.

Hand yourself in. Please.

He covers his mouth and hacks up something, swallows. She puts her tongue between her teeth, grimaces, and heads into the kitchen. The sucky sound of the fridge door opening. Cupboard doors banging. She returns with a glass of orange juice and a packet of paracetamol and ibuprofen.

Take two now. Put the rest in your pocket.

She sits back down, watching him pop and swallow the tablets and down the juice and then place the glass on the side. His hands are shaking but his breathing settles.

When she speaks again her voice is quiet, You need cash?

He appears to be structuring a sentence in his head, turning his gaze towards the curtains, to the sound of the weather encroaching. He can't bring himself to look at her any more. He doesn't want to sleep in the van tonight. He wants to stay here with her, something crosshatching inside him. Lust, fear, heartache. He looks pale, drawn, not quite right. He meets her eye. She looks like a pencil sketch, barely there.

He says, I've spent my life burying everything.

What's that supposed to mean?

The days drinking with you in the Ox. They meant the world to me.

She gets to her feet, rummages in her handbag and passes him some cash.

Please go, she says.

Parked cars, slanting sleet, holding onto the metal rail, taking the snicket down between the houses. Haven't you felt this way a thousand times before?

He returns to his van the next morning to find Bear waiting for him. Rust-coloured jacket. Work boots. Oily Levis. More handsome and vital-looking than Jake remembers.

Jake glances up and down the street. How'd you find me?

65

Pretty obvious if you know what you're looking for.

Jake splutters a cough, wipes his beard.

Bear says, You know the reward's gone up?

Reward?

The Monroe's. Fifty grand. Got men tracking you. And his son.

Who?

Lip Monroe. Never heard of him?

No.

Master of hounds.

Fox hunters?

I know some of the kennelmen and whippers-in. They're not just going to hand you in, Jake. They know you're armed.

Jake considers this. Where they looking?

Closer to home. False leads. They pestered Sheila. I told them to back off.

A woman with a couple of small dogs appears at the top of the street. They watch her cross the road and disappear down a driveway.

Bear says, There's a caravan park just up the coast. Jackson Bay. Usually stay there when I come visit. Old friends own it. Won't ask questions. Sheila says you need to sort your chest out. Something abrupt in his gaze as he adds, One condition. You leave Sheila alone.

Jake squints, reading him. Bear takes the dirty rucksack from his shoulder and hands it over. Sheila told me to give you this. Antibiotics. Out of date, but they'll be right.

Tell her thank you.

Soon as you're fit, get away from the coast.

You think?

Yeah, Bear deadpans. I think.

JACKSON BAY

Three days later, he is at the south-facing window of the caravan where he spends far too much time peering down the incline towards the site owners' wooden cabin. Fully expecting the police to turn up. Not sure if he cares a whit anymore. Worried he's dragged Sheila into all of this. Her ailing heart. Her new start ruined. He should hand himself in. And tell them what? Spending his final days in a prison cell. No.

Thoughts like these.

Outside the window, the snowflakes appear suspended in the air, not falling or drifting, just hanging there. The air around here is sweet with snow, the neighbouring beech wood creaking beneath the weight.

He pops one of the antibiotics and two paracetamols in his mouth and drinks some water. Beyond the clutter of snowflakes, he can just make out the yellow square of the couple's window. Be night soon. Temperature descending with the dark, screwing down upon the site above Jackson Bay, an Arctic blast scouring the coastline. But his food is starting to run out. Never miss the water until the well runs dry. He's seen the scutter of rabbits out in the field at dawn but he doesn't want to push it with these strangers.

The following morning there's a knock at the door.

A man's voice: Time to leave. You hear me?

Jake clears his throat. I hear you.

He swings his legs from the bed and pushes the caravan door open. The blue of the sky—blue of a robin's egg—hurts his eyes. There's no one there.

He knows he should drive inland, west to Wensleydale, hide in the landscape he knows, but he drives down to North Bay hoping to see Sheila one last time.

Scrim of sea-fret, otherworldly curtain hanging across the beach, but a wind is getting up, a sense the tide is retreating out there. Moving down to the tide-line over tangles of kelp and wrack, pop of skate and dogfish cases. The wind is so much stronger now, lifting the fret, clearing it. Distantly he can just make out a tractor dragging a coble across the sand. Then the whole of North Bay opens up, the brightly coloured beach chalets vivid against the jut of headland, the castle silhouetted atop.

Scarborough Castle stands out to sea,
Whitby rocks lyin' northerly.
Oh, what a windy night!

A sound.

Just to the north of him, a girl in an orange puffa jacket sprints towards the waves, chasing a golden cocker spaniel.

Whitecaps scatter, foam streaks.

He moves towards the tide-line, boots sinking into wet sand.

Recalling the summers coming to the resort with Edith and William—ice cream and guesthouses, a blanket on the sun-worn beach. Thinking about the year the lad changed. Anxiety, the doctor reckoned, but William was only eight—what the hell could he be anxious about? He started becoming irritable and clingy, pacing the cottage at night because he couldn't sleep or when he did sleep it was the bedwetting and screaming. Everything on a knife edge. What ifs. Catastrophe. Taking days off school because he couldn't face going in, crying and yelling and so Jake started taking him to work with him. But then it was the farm machinery that scared him, or the sounds of cattle at the auction mart. Distracting him, telling him what he was feeling was normal, that Jake understood. Though he didn't. Then William appeared to have no appetite. For Edith, this was the last straw. It was a long time before they found out what triggered it: overhearing someone talking about farrowing crates and the reason they're used: to stop the sows eating their sucklings. William's young mind filled with the horrors of cannibalism. Jake found stroking him helped. He would close his eyes like a cat being nuzzled and start to breathe deeply and when he came around he would be in something like a trance. Stroking the lad's hair, inhaling his scalpy, cordite smell. Counting the freckles on his face.

Edith: A face without freckles is like a sky without stars.

Then one day it just stopped. It was half-term and William asked if they could go over to Scarborough. He'd heard about the long-rope skipping on Pancake Day. The change in him was sudden. He didn't stop talking the whole way—something that would usually annoy them both but they just kept looking at each other and smiling. William was the first to spot the sea that day and demanded a treat. He joined in with the other children skipping along the Foreshore, desperate to hold the old fishing ropes. Jake kept an eye on him while Edith played bingo in the arcades. Afterwards they sat together in the Sea Cadets'. Sweaty and red-faced, William chelped between bites of hungry skippers with pancakes. Later, they drove to Robin Hood's Bay where Jake bought him a hammer and chisel and that's when the lad's passion for fossils began. Those endless blissful days on the beach. Those indestructible bonds.

The lad was sharp as a tack and the fossil hunting triggered an interest in skeletons and physiology and then husbandry or becoming a vet. It made sense. The drawer beneath his bed was full of boxes, each one containing a 'collection': a box of animal bones he'd gathered when he was out with Jake foraging. Stones he believed had magical qualities. Hair from Jake and Edith's hairbrushes. Receipts from shops. Balls made from elastic bands. A collection of fruit stickers. And now his tiny fossil fragments and a burgeoning fascination with animals. He started disappearing on the farms and Jake would find him trying to coax a feral cat, or smothering the working dogs with kisses. One time he found him curled up asleep in the collies' kennel with a puppy. And he'd just started his science A-levels when.

About to venture out into the world when.

About to plough his own furrow when.

When.

The scroll of waves mimics Jake's pulse, ebb and flow dragging pebbles and sand, misery and regret. Across the shelf of the sea Jake stares, feeling shipwrecked. This coast is his heart, the waves its liquid pulse. The itch of tears on his cheeks. Pain is all he has left of them now.

The clouds sunder, throwing light down into the waves. He closes his eyes, inhales the sea's depths. Gulls slice the air with their skrikes. A dog barks. A girl shouts.

That sound.

Opening his eyes, he sees the girl and her dog being dragged into the sea, unseen rip taking them away. There is no one around. Stumbling over the rocks into the cold mouth of the water, he hesitates, knowing this will lead to his capture. He peers back along the beach. No one. The girl bobs beneath the surface and then up again. He wades into the lumpy water, struggling to stay upright. He pulls off his parka. She is flailing further out. Beneath the surf the shock of the freezing water is so complete, saltwater boiling around him as he struggles against the sea's momentum, rising high, searching for purchase on the pitted slope of rock, shale, shifting sand. She is tumbling, a wave catching her and bringing her nearer. He grasps the hood of her jacket. Their bodies sway, lift, drop. Dragging her backwards, fist like a grappling hook, the sea draws past them both in a whoosh. He digs his heels in but she is pulling him down, consuming him with ocean sounds. He drags and drags with all his might, saltwater in his mouth as he shouts, Come on.

Soon, they are out of the waves and he drops onto his knees in the sand.

That's it.

A woman's shouts growing nearer. The girl is spewing water and reaching for the dog. Chubby fish-white girl in an orange puffa jacket and rainbow moonboots.

That's it.

And the woman is here, all around her. He searches the waves—nowt but surf.

Thank you oh my god thank you thank you.

The mother's haunted expression. People rushing towards them across the sands. He retrieves his parka sloshing in the shallows.

The woman saying, What's your name?

A boy is pointing his mobile phone at the girl. Jake turns his back. The distant sound of a siren.

What's your name?

Guard her, Jake says.

What?

With your life.

He steps out of his body. Takes one juddering step in front of the other. Jake watching Jake walk away, cold as a dead fish, sunk in some kind of dream.

BROXA

He pulls into the side of the road, climbs into the back of the van, peels off his sopping all-weather gear and changes into dry clothes. He is experiencing something like vertigo, the ambiguous almost-loss of a girl he doesn't even know. Mind unmoored, his breathing has a hysterical hitch. Struggling to rub the sand off his skin and pull the pair of fresh socks over his crinkled feet, his limbs begin to shake again, his extraordinary stamina beginning to wane. Outside the van door a group of thrushes are feasting on the blood-red berries of a holly bush. He reads the scene as an augur of ill fate, wondering if anyone saw his number plate as he pulled away from the beach. Did any cameras pick him up?

He gets into the driver's seat and steers into the hills, the van feeling sluggish, juddering on bends and at low speeds. Driving westward for another twenty minutes before the van eventually stalls outside the village of Broxa. The needle says empty and the fuel warning light is on.

Happen the float level has stuck?

He tries to picture himself standing on the beach, wondering what he was thinking about before the girl got sucked into the waves. The sea-fret. The castle. The brightly coloured chalets. He can't remember. Instead he is staring at his left hand and realises something is missing. Eyeing his ring finger, pale band of skin. His wiggles his finger. His wedding ring has gone. The sea has it. Mind blank, he rests his head against the steering wheel and almost sobs. So be it. Gathering his things together, he checks he still has the photograph of William on him before setting off on foot. An easterly is rising, making a sound through the nearby trees like a snide whisper. He rubs his chill-reddened ears and wraps his arms around himself. The sleet comes. Another hour or two until sunset. Never quit. Soon he can make out a church steeple above the trees. Just a hiker cutting across the fell if anyone cares to see.

Sweating but half-frozen, he enters the warmth of the church through the transept door. At the far end of the nave an ensemble of singers is standing in the wooden choir—twenty-or-so men and women of different ages, clasping hymn sheets. The organist at his console below the tall ranks of metal pipes. No one pays Jake any heed as he shuffles into the shadows and crowds a radiator for warmth. His breathing settles. The conductor waves his hands and the organist plays a sequence of solemn chords and the choir begins to sing. Such grace and passion and majesty colouring Jake's blood. Something about the nave, the ornate columns inclined and branched, remind him of the Outwoods, of Edith and William and Charles and everything that led up to this moment, seeking shelter in a remote church somewhere on the North York Moors.

The area next to Jake is sectioned off with a long dark curtain—the vicar's tiring house. As the singing intensifies he pulls the curtain aside and enters the gloom. He removes the damp clothes from the bin bag, spreading them out to dry on the lukewarm radiator. He drains the last of his water bladder and unfurls his roll mat behind a large mahogany writing desk. Be safe here for a while, hidden. Stepping into his sleeping

73

bag he settles himself down beneath an embroidered sign:

DID I TELL YOU THAT JESUS LOVES YOU?

Bothering the skin on his ring finger with his thumb. Fifty-two years rubbed smooth.

He judders awake and palms the sleep from his eyes. He's sweating. What time is it? The church is semi-lit. A door rattles in the wind. He pulls on his damp, foul-smelling boots and peers from behind the curtain. Footsteps. A voice: Hello? A vicar and an old woman appear. They look embarrassed for a reason Jake can't intuit.

Sorry, the vicar says.

Jake nods, regarding them dully.

The old woman says, Didn't want to wake you.

The vicar: It's you?

Saved that lass this morning?

They said on TV.

We thought.

A searing in Jake's guts. No, he says.

The woman's smile fading, something like sadness running from her body.

Jake retreats into the tiring house, pulls on his trapper hat, scarf and gloves, takes his clothes from the radiator and shoves them into his backpack, dragging it up onto his shoulders, skin sore along the strap lines.

They are still there.

Sorry, Jake says.

Wait, they say.

The night outside is still and strangely mild. He moves between the ragged teeth of headstones to the far edge of the graveyard where he drops his trousers and empties his guts in the darkness, a rasp and suck through gritted teeth. A ferric smell. Blood? He pulls up his trousers and moves away between the graves, the pack like a wet bale on his back. He pushes forward, through the wooden lychgate and into a field, his damp boots and socks gnawing at his feet, raising blisters. In the middle of the field he slumps forwards and massages the cramp from his thighs. How far has he travelled from Scarborough? Not far enough. Tongues wagging, TV, the ebb and flow of rumours. Lip Monroe, the men, the police— they'll see the mobile phone footage of him on the beach and know.

Fifty grand? Was that all it was worth?

Lip Monroe, Master of Hounds. Fox hunters: terrier men on quads, pony clubbers in hacking jackets, car horns and bugle calls—those privileged hooligans.

Your father had it coming.

Oh, yes, my love has listed and I for him will rove,
I'll write his name on every tree that grows in yonder grove,
Where the huntsman he do holler and the hounds do sweetly cry,
To remind me,
To remind me,
To remind me,
To remind me,
To remind me of me ploughboy until the day I die.

He couldn't fathom the fact they hadn't tracked him yet. A man killed your father—at what point are you going to quit hunting him down? Never. Happen they thought only an idiot would head directly home and they were searching the coastline. Or the owners of the petrol station outside Whitby saw his face on TV, phoned the police and put them off the scent, repeating Jake's tale about spending Christmas with his fictional daughter in Redcar.

He pictures the men tracking him, bending over, studying his cleat marks in the dirt, squinting at the spoor where Jake has trampled through bushes and low-hanging branches, recreating his journey west, the impressions of his boots revealing his gait, deducing he has blisters on both feet and a heavy pack on his back.

Cutting across a field he realises the dark shapes are a fold of Highland cattle lying down. He continues towards the nearby woodland, half-expecting to see the moon-shadows of men among the trees. He needs to gather his thoughts, gumption. Mouthing silent words, he works out a metre in his head, keeping pace with it, the noise of all that happened on the beach flexing behind him, but each step towards the trees spells out his utter aloneness in the world. This unforeseen, abrupt and aching need to return to Dove Cottage. Just one more night in his own bed, that's all. Then they can do what they want.

He pauses. An engine noise in the clouds above. The whump and wash of a chopper's rotor blades. Must be a police helicopter, this time of night? Thermal imaging cameras. He turns back on himself, slowly approaching the cattle at the field's edge. A sentinel cow with long fine horns watches him. A bull beside her galumphs to his feet. Jake sits down among them, among the sweetness of their breaths, singing softly:

E bowt 'er twenty good milk kye,
She let nineteen o' them go dry.
She only milked 'er once a year,
An' that was ti mak butter dear...

DALBY FOREST

Two hours ago, vehicles striped the forest with headlights. Men's voices, distant. Jake rubs the frost from his iron-grey beard, thinking about something Bear said last week. What was he intimating? That they knew Jake was armed? Claim killing him was an act of self-defence? Lip Monroe punishing the working-class man for killing his father.

Does Lip know William was his half-brother?

A muntjac starts calling, a sound similar to the young girl in the waves skriking for her dog. Then all is quiet.

Beneath the mill's old roof timbers, he lights the stove and squeezes some water into the mess tin, waiting as it comes to a boil. Removes his boots, gingerly peels off his socks and washes his feet with some of the hot water. Runs the tip of his hunting knife through the stove's flame, pierces the edge of his blisters. Presses out the fluid. Then he tips the rest of the water over. Using the back of his spoon against a rock he squashes a clove of garlic and rubs it over the blisters to disinfect them. Then he tears another strip from the hem of a thermal top and gaffa tapes it over the blisters, placing his feet next to the stove to warm up. Recalling the summers shearing all day, hessian moccasins, stench of lanolin and Maggot Oil.

The fever has passed but his eyes and nose continue to leak and there is a twisting gripe to his guts. He thinks about the smell of blood that came from him amid the gravestones yesterday and he reasons he injured himself when he was in the waves with the girl. Then he thinks about how much food he has left. The rabbit he killed and skinned out at dawn. The puffball he'd cut into strips and smoke-dried. The navelwort he'd picked from a drystone wall to aid his stomach. Handful of spruce needles for tea. Two days' worth of food, maybe three. But rabbit was no good. You could starve to death on rabbit. He needed fatty meat, another goose or young squirrel, but he was loath to leave the mill just yet. Planning to wait for nightfall before heading out. But he is spooked by a dog barking close by.

He collects his things and makes his way out of the forest, gyring up onto the moor beside drystone walls. Images of his thoughts unite with his footfalls. Recalling their honeymoon weekend in Liverpool, sitting on a bench watching the sun go down. How he kept having to wipe his palms on his trousers.

He thought he'd left such thoughts behind but it's as if the more he walks the more such thoughts return, each step untethering new memories, rising to the surface and bursting with feral power.

Edith's father had big ideas for his daughter and they didn't involve falling in love with a lad like Jake. He'd cut her out of the will if they continued to mess around. Jake wanted to go over to Sedbergh, find the bastard and knock him out.

Then Edith suggested they tie the knot.

Mam thinks we should get wed, she said.

Wed?

Aye. That thing folk do before they get divorced.

Lizzie is so easy led,
The' say that 'e takes 'er to bed,
She used to be skinny, nah look at 'er pinny,
Ah think it's 'baht time the' were wed.

Are you expecting?

No. Unfortunately.

When he didn't respond, she added, I always fancied a spring wedding.

You'd need rocks in your head to want to marry me.

Her father told her she would never again be welcome at his home. Edith thought it was hilarious.

Their mams met in Kendal for afternoon tea and seemed to get on OK. Edith's mam—a woman as meek as a leveret—visited them regularly and helped out financially with the cottage. Jake's father was in the final stages of Parkinson's, the knobbled hooks of his forever-shaking hands grasping at his end-days, so that bastard's opinion didn't matter a whit. They had the prescribed visit to the church and homily from the vicar who clearly knew less about married life than they did, but the vicar said something Jake didn't intuit because as they left the church Edith said she'd prefer the registry office.

Jake was close to his two older sisters and thought he was canny when it came to womenfolk and their ways. The three of them were together all of the time as kids, brown as berries all summer, cycling to their little secret cave behind a foss near Aysgarth. They used to huddle behind the curtain of water and make plans about running away. Waiting until dark because Father was usually passed out by then. Mam would pour them lemonade and they would eat supper in the yard. His sisters thought he was in a world of his own but he was paying close attention to every cadence and subtext, whatever their gestures might belie.

By the time he met Edith, both of his sisters had married and moved

79

away—Amy to Durham and Mary to Carlisle. But when they heard the news they took it upon themselves to visit Sedbergh and do some digging into Edith's past.

Why do you think she's still single, Jacob?

The argument, the name-calling—it stung his heart. But he wasn't even sure if he could frame his questions or even articulate his doubts because deep down, he simply didn't care. He was just happy she was his, fettered to her no matter what.

The long list of wedding guests ended up being just a few bums on seats. Edith's daffy sister making a scene, though Jake couldn't perceive any handicap, just a spoilt woman-child who craved attention. Then there was the buffet and free bar in the side room at the Comrades Club. Edith didn't seem to mind that it was a small do or that hardly any of her family turned up. In fact, he'd never seen her happier, flitting around with a glass of Cherry B in her hand, laughing louder than everyone else.

That long drive down to Liverpool. Jake had never been to a hotel before. Awkward and embarrassed, he wasn't even sure what to do at the reception desk. But Edith took over things and made him feel like an even bigger fool because being married meant you were an adult and surely adults know how to do such things. They were only on the other side of the country but it felt like a foreign land. The lit-up noise and litter and grime. The bizarre accent and the comings and goings of the staff in the corridors. The hotel at the end of Hope Street overlooking the Anglican Cathedral, an intimidating crag face so huge it absorbed the light. In the near distance the coffee-coloured Mersey. Beyond that, the mountains of north Wales, late spring snow clinging to the peaks. The smell of cigarette smoke and cooking in the room. A forgotten pair of leather gloves in the rickety wardrobe. Then there was the indignity of the evening meal in the dining room. Jake didn't even know which cutlery to use or the correct custom for tipping the waiter. Edith was impetuous with the staff, obstinate, even, the privilege of her upbringing coming out.

He was glad they hadn't waited to have sex. He was already familiar with the constellation of moles on her back and the hair around her belly button (like goose down) and the birthmark inside her thigh (three bilberries). For Jake their first night together as man and wife was more about waking up beside her, watching her in the morning light in her negligée, massaging her hands in front of the window, her body silhouetted, fingers slick with her favourite cinnamon lotion—knowing full well the effect it would have on him. He snapped the bedsheets back. Howay.

The Mersey was full of sailing ships for the Tall Ships Regatta. Sitting on a bench watching the sun set over the Wirral, Edith told him a story about her eldest brother, how he ran away to sea when he was a young lad and sailed the world until he died. She never met him, only knew him from old letters and photographs. But something about the way she delivered the story—an almost mournful longing for the kind of life Jake could never confer.

Distant gunshot. Discharge of a 12-bore echoing through the hills. Jake peers around. Heart pulsing, he tells himself it's nowt. Just a farmer's propane cannon. Bird scarer.

He pinches the bridge of his nose, discharges an oyster of snot.

Come on.

Upwelling and dipping until he crests the plateau, feeling the roughly hewn land of rock and turf around him, he looks about—just a few gimmers and ewes, black-faced Swaledales, fleece the colour of piss. He follows the way signs until he comes to a ramshackle farm. The place looks deserted. Listening cautiously, he's skirting the front yard when two collies shoot out of their kennels, lunging on hind legs, chains tight, teeth snapping. Heart in his throat he moves back into the field and descends through a steep alder carr to a fast-running beck. He removes the pack and rests a while, stretching the burn from his limbs, trying to ignore the pain in his feet. Working out where he is. Levisham Beck? No. He would have crossed the road to Whitby by now.

He still has a half-hour of daylight left, and other than the sound of the orange-tinged water he can't hear a thing. He sips from the water bladder watching a fish kiss the surface of the beck. Tiny haloes.

Setting off downstream, along the sandy bank pocked with rabbit warrens burrowed between exposed tree roots. Paw prints in the mud, badger, water rat. Soon he comes to a clearing at the bottom of a deep ghyll. He slumps into the grass, wriggles free of the pack, sits up and presses the scabs on his knees. The spot is isolated, no stiles or livestock around. The ground above the beck levels off enough to pitch a tent. Though he knows the frost will arrive hard and early here in the ghyll. He'll fill his water bladder and light a small fire and have a good feed, force dry the remaining meat over the smoke. Planning to set off before dawn, switching into his new routine of night-walking and day-sleeping.

Groggy, three or four hours before dawn, he takes the tent down and folds it into the compression sack and shoulders the pack. Squinting up into the creamy wheel of stars he finds Hydra pointing south-west. Good enough. He places a red sock over his torch to see better in the dark, stepping slow and careful into the circle of pinkish light. Soon he is into open farmland and spots the yellow tunnels of a pair of headlights moving towards the A170, his route west. He has a vague idea he is just to the north of Thornton-le-Dale. He switches off the torch, placing it in the pack's side pocket, a sudden waft of garlic from his hands and feet. The flat open country is easier to see peripherally, off-centre, studying the ground below him through his eye corners.

Close by: a vehicle on the road, slowing, pulling in.

Hands out before him, he gets onto his knees, crouching low to the icy ground, a hare in a form. Have they seen him? Voices. Music. But it's just a man relieving himself against a hedge. Jake waits for the car to move off again before getting to his feet and continuing, sighing into the half-formed dawn.

Crossing a stile, he trundles into the next field, socks rucking against his blisters. Now he knows where he is. 70 or 75 miles away from home. That's all.

You took your ruddy time.

He askèd him for some relief,
And said with tears of seeming grief,
That she had neither house nor home,
But for her living was forced to roam.

He spots a wooden hut, a bird hide, about 50 metres away. He moves over to a stand of laurel, stumbling in between the leaves, takes the binoculars from his pack and glasses the land. Sparkle of frost. Silks of mist in the lower fields. Silver flash of fieldfares. His haunches shiver. Breathing heat into his gloves, a maw of hunger snails his brain, his stomach making deep quacking sounds. He inhales, clenches his gloved fists, releases a groan.

Fuck it. He breaks cover and trots across the field.

Scuffing his boots over the door jamb, scraping off the mud and frost, the bird hide is bare inside apart from a few RSPB posters on the wall. He props the pack against the door, removes his gloves and trapper hat and runs his fingers through his hair. He steps over to the window. Nowt. He lowers the shutter a fraction and then removes his boots and socks and the gaffa tape, examining his feet in the half-light as the water boils. He squeezes some garlic over them and lets them air. Then he makes some needle tea and eats some of the rabbit meat and herbs. Hunger sated, the hide heating up nicely, he cleans the rifle and magazine and then steps into his sleeping bag. Notices the sign on the wall.

Please:
Talk and move quietly
Do not lean or reach beyond the windows
Make room for newcomers

Do not smoke
Take litter home

The faint sound of the wind outside, distant accompaniment, the material of the sleeping bag so warm, so soft against his face, easing him into sleep. He sees the girl again, orange parka bobbing on the coffee-coloured sea, her mam's voice—*who are you?*—whispering through his dreams...

She swam until she floated unto the river's brim,
The old man took his walking stick and shoved her farther in.

He blinks up at the wooden roof of the hide. All he can hear is his heart and then the men's voices. He clambers over to the window and raises the shutter an inch. Two men higher up the field, one with a tan lurcher on a leash, the other a shotgun cracked over his arm. They are a few metres apart, gesticulating.

Is this it?

Is Jake equal to this?

Quickly he gathers his belongings and pulls on his boots and goes to the window again. He can't see them. He stumbles his way down the field, the undone laces on his boots gathering frost, the sky down on its hunkers, baring its teeth. He realises he is completely exposed, scanning the empty landscape as he stumbles across the land. Soon he comes to a beck too wide to cross and no way is he getting his boots wet again. He enters a copse and drops his trousers and empties his guts, listening to the swish of traffic on the main road.

Unaware of the man in the distance watching.

Five months earlier

THE COMMUNITY HOSPITAL

He parked at the side of the Ox and headed into the snug. The barmaid came to the hatch with a look on her face.

She said, Haven't you heard?

What?

Sheila's in hospital, Jake. Collapsed this morning.

A fog came down in his mind. He saw his son, William, lying on the grass in the park, boys gathered around.

Jake? You hear me?

He left it four days before he went to visit her. She had a room to herself and was fast asleep. In a green wing-back chair he sat observing her. Then he cleared his throat again and coughed. She blinked awake, sat up.

How long you been here? she said.

Not long.

She tugged the bed sheet over her nightgown and smoothed her hair.

He said, You looked champion when I saw you last.

She drank some water from a plastic cup and said she'd pieced it all together.

I was heading to Bear's and just came over all queer like. This pain—a hand to her throat—like fire. You know me, sometimes I get all out of puff and a fag helps clear my chest. I know. Was rummaging in my bag when I stumbles. Lucky I didn't get sodding run over.

He watched her talk, animated.

She said, And don't you want to know what the strangest thing was? What?

My cardiac. It was the loudest sound I've ever heard. Like bomb going off.

The wind got up sudden and loud outside the room, hiss of rain falling in the hospital grounds. They both glanced towards the pane. Then Jake reached over and squeezed her hand.

She said, They want me to go to something called cardio rehab. An exercise program and this talking group thingamajig. Codswallop. Have to change my diet and keep a weight journal and look at stress reduction. Stress? Only way I can avoid stress is to leave bloody town. Karen and that frigging bairn screaming the house down. Said I need bed-rest. Ha! Chance would be a fine thing. Eat less meat, more fish. But a life without butter and cheese? Are they effing mad?

Jake eyed the heart monitor and said, I'd—

What?

I'd suggest staying at mine. It's just—

He pictured the state of Dove Cottage. Traces of Edith everywhere. Damp. Isolation.

That's very sweet of you, she said. But—

At that moment a young woman came into the room. Scraggly hair. Too-tight cardigan. Her skin looked like a pair of net curtains that had been hanging in an abandoned house.

Sheila sighed and said, Karen, Jake, Jake, Karen.

Karen folded her arms, face split with a look. This your mystery fella then? Bit old, isn't he?

Sheila said, Watch your lip.

Jake stood up. I best—

No, Sheila said. Sit yourself down.

Jake retook his seat.

Sheila glanced at the heart monitor and then pointed at Karen. You heard what the doc said about stressing me out. Now sod off home and give us some peace. Go on!

Karen cursed and left the room.

A burning silence followed.

MONROE HALL

The narrow road laced over the moor, the quad buzzing through isolated villages, the sort with only two surnames in the graveyard. In just under a half an hour he arrived at the gatehouse, a triumphal arch at the easterly edge of the country estate. A sign warned of livestock grazing. Keeping the quad in second, he passed beneath the arch and over the cattle grid, puttering along a driveway lined with ancient oaks transected by sharp morning light. Amid the flickering trees, Hebridean ewes and three-month-old lambs were grazing. He passed a couple of tree surgeons in their orange helmets and ear defenders smoking by the side of their truck. They nodded at Jake and Jake touched his cap brim. Gradually the trees thinned and he was out into the light. Below him: sweeping lawns, vast yew hedges, a kidney-shaped lake curving beneath the vast Hall. Imagining Edith living here. Some happier parallel life.

He didn't know how long she had been messing around with Charles. Six, seven months maybe. When did they meet? Did she know him through her father? Connections between the Monroes and Willoughbys over in the west of the county? But Jake saw the article in the local paper: Charles had got engaged to a young woman in the Lakes who came from titled nobility. Jake knew what it meant: their union would lift the Monroes from mere landed gentry to true aristocracy. Edith was out of the picture. He assumed that was why she had become so taciturn and snappy lately.

He eyed the north face of the magnificent Monroe Hall. Such places sickened him with what they represented: generations of downtrodden poor in the factories and mill-towns. Claggy-arsed industry, scab of the North Country.

I've seen grey fog creep ovver Leeds Brig as thick as Bastille soup,
I've lived where folks have been stowed away like rabbits in a coop,
I've seen snow float down Bradford Beck as black as ebony.
From Hunslet, Holbeck, Wibsey Slack, good Lord deliver me.

Recalling the stone tied-cottage of his childhood. Two rooms. Earth floor. Hardly any furniture. Bed sheets made from scraps of old clothes. Cold, near starvation. Carrying water from the well. Bathing in the beck. Father pissing their money away, his baritone singing waking them at night.

From Brig o' Dread when thou may'st pass.
To Purgatory fire thou com'st at last...

Often-fierce Mam. Sisters married off young.

His parents were forced to work at fourteen to support their families and so his mam was over the moon when he won a place at grammar school. He'd never have to slog his guts out for a paltry wage. No, he could use his nouse! Father moaning about the price of the uniform, calling Jake a 'Little Tory'.

Coots, swans and Canada geese floated across the lid of the lake. A tractor driving across a nearby field being mobbed by rooks. A couple of overdressed hikers ambling by, wishing Jake a chirpy good morning. Behind him, the bleats of lambs emerging from the shade.

Howay.

Jake headed over the bridge, along the sweeping driveway towards the National Trust office. Hesitating in the doorway, he stepped inside.

Hanging at the rear of a group of surprisingly well-behaved children in public school uniforms, boys sporting blazers and ties and girls in tunic dresses and pinafores. Wandering the wide echoing halls and gloomy rooms, galleries of opulence and antiquity, paintings of still lives and hunting scenes.

The group entered a small book-lined room and it was here Jake saw the painting above the enormous fireplace. Charles Monroe, his face returning to Jake through the years.

Since he has been the only cause
Of my sorrow, grief and woe...

Jake glanced away then back again.

In the painting the ennobled Charles was wearing a long dark greatcoat, hands clasped in front of him, and Jake couldn't deny it: Charles' face was William's face. Even the colouring of his eyes—amber, often bright orange.

Inheriting his blood father's shadow.

Recalling William at fourteen months old, how he began to change. There was no way anyone could say he resembled Jake anymore, not with that carrot top. And yet William was such a daddy's boy, always reaching out and skriking for Jake whenever he fell or hurt himself. And the lad would stand up to him and answer him back—his father's comportment, no doubt. But he had the cheekiest of grins, and those dimples! Worried the lad would turn out to be a handful. How could he discipline a lad that wasn't his own? Worried how far he would push him. Worried about his capacity for patience, love. Would the lad know? Sense some difference? Would a gap open up between them and create a split in the family unit? But William became lanky, loving, sweet-natured, funny. Jake adored him.

The tour guide's voice snapped Jake into the present, the group moving into another room.

Jake's parting glance at Charles Monroe.

He shouldn't have come here.

Beneath the narrow archway leading out of the country estate, Jake noticed an old man in the garth observing him. The man raised a hand. Jake squeezed the front brake and cut the engine.

Jake ruddy Eisner, Jonjo said. Not seen you for donkeys. How you keeping?

Middling. Thissen?

Can't complain.

Jonjo resembled a bird of prey. The whole family were the same: narrow heads, swarthy skin, hook-nebbed.

The two men nodded in compliance.

Jake says, You work here?

Nigh on twenty years. He launched into a story about the trouble he was having with a badger sett near the hermitage. Did Jake see?

No. Just been into the Hall like. For the tour.

Jonjo squinting at him—*Right*—as if a bloke like Jake would travel all this way to look around some posh twat's gaff.

Jake hooked a thumb over his shoulder. Ever come over yon moor?

Now and then.

Know the Ox?

Not been in years.

I'm there Sunday if you fancy a feed?

Might just do that.

Grand.

Jonjo raised a palm. Sorry about—

Jake nodded.

Edith, Jonjo said. Cracking lass.

He followed the road back over the moor and found himself pulling into a passing-place beside the reservoir. He cut the engine and placed his feet on the ground, removed his cap and ran his fingers through his hair.

Jonjo. He was among the group of young men propping up the bar that night—the night Jake and Edith first danced. All those eyes watching him, unsure what to make of the spectacle. Not the fact that Jake wasn't shuffling in his patent leathers like the rest of the crowd—jiving and twisting to the five-piece covers band—but that he was doing a quickstep full of syncopations.

Jake eyed the corbelled sides of the iron-grey reservoir wall.

Silence.

Then above him: a hawk's killy and stoop, the only movement and sound for miles around.

He gasped awake, turned on the bedside lamp and scanned his lonely room. Rust-coloured water stains on the wall. Candlesticks on the mantelpiece, candles burned to the nub. Green tub chair strewn with clothes. He shuffled over to Edith's side of the bed, sniffing at the peach-coloured fabric of the headboard.

Recalling their first dance again. And here she comes...

Do you really want to be doing this? said the voice of Edith in his head.

Doing what?

Getting all mushy. Sentimental like.

Oh shush.

Shush thissen.

Until that moment no one had really heard the music inside him and he was convinced the roof of the dancehall opened up that night, his blood whirring steady and hot like a furnace, beads of sweat popping along his brow. Edith had the biggest grin on her face, frequently breaking into laughter, and they were spinning so fast their hips kept glancing, the burn of lust in his eyes. She didn't seem to notice how drunk he was, though she was obviously surprised by how nimble he was on his feet.

The song finished and they stood gawping at each other, breathing hard. She suggested they go outside together for a cigarette and he told her he didn't smoke and she said, It's about time I quit anyway.

She held out her arms as the next song began.

The click of her heels on the wooden floor, flare and whoosh of her skirt, swell of her breasts, smell of her perfume and hair and something else, something dusty and leathery and oily, the pale stem of her neck revealed by her chignon hairdo, her long fine fingers in his peasant hands. They spun and spun around each other's hearts but the song finished too soon and she looked at her naked wrist and said, Is that the time? You can pick me up tomorrow. I'm staying—

I know where it is.

Course you do. One pm. Don't be late.

She patted his arm and frowned, though more at herself it seemed, and then turned and weaved her way through the dancers and into his life.

THE OX

Jonjo was a slow eater and had the habit of whistling when his mouth wasn't full. Whistling prat. And he was one of those old sods that liked to chelp about the good old days. Jake thinking: fuck the good old days.

Jake stood up. Another pint?

The barmaid asked how Sheila was getting on.

On the mend.

She out yet?

Been home a few days. Popping to see her tomorrow.

Send her my regards.

Jake glanced over at Jonjo, rehearsing the lines in his head. Then he took the drinks over, sat down and just came out with it.

So, Charles Monroe?

Him.

Still alive?

Half-dead more like.

Why's that?

Stroke, Jonjo said. Knocked the stuffing out of him. One side limp like a ragdoll. Trouble talking.

Jake's thoughts detouring to the week after William's death when they thought William's heart condition might point to something congenital. Hundred per cent blockage of the left anterior descending. The widow-maker, the doctor called it. Would Jake mind having tests done? No, he said, and performed that particularly bleak impersonation one more time.

Jonjo adds, He's in a private nursing home near Wappentake. Family own the place. Moved the entire village? Rebuilt it brick by brick a mile north. Was ruining their view... What's up?

Nowt, Jake said with such a crooked smile.

In the kitchen, door open wide, whittling the peel from an apple in one long curl, eyeing the sodden moor, grass heads bent by the recent shower, wind chucking his shirt collar under his chin, palming hair from his face, mulling Charles' debility, picturing paper-smocked nurses and technicians attending to him, blood tests and syringe changes and brain graphing, all that wealth and privilege and here you are, reduced to this.

Oh, may he never prosper and may he never thrive,
In everything he takes a hand as long as he's alive...

Jake got his splitting maul and went out into the storm, chopping into the old oak block, singing at the top of his lungs. He was soon drenched but he kept swinging the maul high, bringing it down dead centre of each log.

May the very grass he treads upon the ground refuse to grow,
Since he has been the,

Since he has been the,
Since he has been the,
Since he has been the,
Since he has been the only cause of my sorrow, grief and woe.

Wiping the rain from his taut arms and chest, a feeling came over him. One he'd not experienced since William was alive. He went back inside to drink more whiskey, watching the land change. Pretty soon the rumbling began. Death seemed to be drifting across the moor right then, filling every pore with rotten winds. More thunder, flat reports like rifle shots, summits floodlit in flickering light.

He barely slept that night. Insects tapping around the room, windows wide, listening to the martins. He'd stood in the garden in the blush of the approaching sunset watching them hovering and feeding the chicks. A few days earlier he'd seen the chicks coming out for the first time, testing their wings.

Dawn. He grabbed a blanket and wrapped it around his shoulders, coming down the stairs in his pyjamas. Outside, drawing the burn of morning air into his lungs, he smelt the rain coming. Eyeing the thin wash of colour above the horizon, two bands of yellow and blue creating a tension over the landscape. He pulled himself out and arched a long hot piss into the air.

Charles, the story he set in motion, carrying Jake along inside it, thrashing against its walls for forty-six years.

William's funeral, Charles beneath the sycamore kicking weeds at his feet, half-looking, something like defiance on his face, like he had every right to be there and it was Jake who was trespassing. But there was something else behind Charles' gaze. Something Jake recognised. Something that made him very uneasy.

See you soon, Jake said.

The *kronk* of a corvid echoed across the moor.

Jake shook his cock and headed back in.

Later that morning: a noise coming from the back garden. Bloody fox again, no doubt. Raggedy-arsed fox with his injured hind paw hopping around the bins.

Reynard, you bastard.

Another noise, a clatter. The sound of knocking. Sheila's voice coming through the letterbox, startling him.

Jake? You in there? Jake?

The wallop of his heart.

Why didn't he answer? He needed company right now.

He eyed the damp in the far corner making the wall glow, chartreuse of mould climbing between curls of wallpaper, making colours he'd never seen before.

She shouted, I know you're in there!

Was there some truth in what her daughter said? Your mystery fella. Is that what Sheila thought? Is that what she'd been telling folk?

Felt like he was betraying Edith in some way.

I've left some shopping by the door. Call me!

Downstairs, he paused to listen to Edith in the kitchen. Faintly she hummed along to the radio. Then her voice: *Brew?*

He smiled. Cheers, flower.

He headed into the living room, morning light falling aslant through the curtains. He planted himself on the settee, picked up his brogues and dribbled a glob of spit down onto the toe, rubbing it in with his short sleeve.

She entered: a motion blur. She often wafted into the room smelling of perfume and hairspray, and here, now, he inhaled the air as she passed him a mug of hot sweet tea, handle first, and then groaned as she took her place beside him.

The dip in the cushions where she used to sit.

Sipped. Sighed. *Grand that*, she said.

Silence.

Are you all right?

No, he said. I'm half left.

Let me go.

The light in the room dimmed. Jake paused, listened. Reaching out with both hands, pushing into the dimness of the room, he felt the walls of his loneliness getting stronger.

Later, wandering around the garden, cup of tea in one hand, the other massaging his neck, at that moment he knew what needed to be done. He went back inside and poured himself a three-finger whiskey. Then he took a coin from his pocket, flipped it into the air and caught it on the back of his hand.

Tails.

Rummaging in the closet under the stairs, moving boxes and old clothes and plastic bags around. He found it. Unzipping the case, enjoying the dark heft of the rifle in his hands, a Ruger 10/22 Takedown. Synthetic stock, threaded muzzle, Burris scope and noise suppressor. Turned out to be the best hunting rifle he ever had—consistent, smooth, super accurate, great in bad weather. Considering its provenance, a retirement gift from Edith, quitting that last farm with such a weight of reluctance, but Edith was nearly 80, worn, addled.

That evening he stood in the garden scanning the distant moor through the scope, reading the late-summer life around him, cross-haired.

MOAT FARM ESTATE

Sheila rolled onto her back and examined the light above her bed, spheres of dust rotating like mini planets. The silence of the house. The curtains were open a crack and clouds passed by in their varied designs. She was due on a nightshift in an hour's time. She closed her eyes, recalling her week in hospital, Karen and Bear at her side, on the edge of things, the strip lights and oxygen, the suction and GTN spray, nurses bringing their needles and looks. The ridiculously handsome consultant had the most beautiful teeth, his skin tanned and flawless, but he looked like an actor performing for an audition, explaining what happened to her, drawing diagrams in the air with his hands. Maybe he'd been told to improve his bedside manner and increase his empathy and the result was this: talking about her body like it was a machine.

If it wasn't for the angioplasty, he said, you'd have suffered permanent damage. You're lucky to be alive, he added. We'll need to do an echocardiogram in the next few days to check the ejection fraction and heart function. Then he muttered something about cardio rehab and asked about the situation at home and immediately she thought about Clem screaming the house down.

Clem, her alien, uninspiring grandson. A couple of weeks ago he was totally doing her head in and she drew a pair of Ming the Merciless eyebrows on his forehead with mascara. The more he cried the more she laughed. He looked hilarious! But the way he carried on. She resented him more than she loved him and she knew it was wrong feeling that way about your kin.

Mam popped in to see her at the hospital every afternoon. She wouldn't sit down, just stand there toying with the buttons on the front of her coat, an undercurrent of something flowing across her face. Sadness? Fear? Kissing Sheila goodbye with her bristly lips.

The following afternoon, pushing the buggy through the steep streets of the estate, handles laden with carrier bags, the bairn quiet for once, she stopped at the top of the rise and sat on a garden wall, picking the blouse from her breasts. Clem opened his eyes. She blew a raspberry at him, making him frown. With his pop-eyes and enormous bonce and rolls of fat—

Ugly little sod, aren't you? Take after your dad, don't you? Don't you? Yes. Yes, you do. Yes!

But then she felt bad, recalling the day Karen had the scan and how everything, in a single moment, changed. Clem's heartbeat over Karen's, the rapid whoosh of new life. How they both cried and then laughed. But the glow only lasted until he released his first gripe and wail. Months later the sound hadn't stopped.

She got to her feet and pushed the buggy home where she found a note on the kitchen table in Karen's scrawl: *Back in a bit*.

Sake.

She checked the fridge and found some formula. Initially, Karen started him on the tit. The way she'd unbutton and get her nipple out no matter where she was—Sheila liked that, and not just because Clem fell so silent. It was the way he clamped on and the quietness that overcame him and the way Karen would hold him at those moments. Sheila remembered all too well the almost orgasmic feeling of breastfeeding. But one of Karen's friends had said something to her, filling her head with guff. Breastfeeding ruins your tits. Deflated balloons. Swinging dugs like an old sow. Or maybe it was that dick-head she was dating.

Clem was starting to whine and kick in his buggy and there was a pong coming from him but he could wait until she was good and ready. She lifted the carrier bags onto the side and restocked the fridge and then made herself a cuppa.

Her thoughts returning to Jake.

Why was the old bugger ignoring her?

Was he ill? Had she upset him?

I'll pop up to Dove Cottage again in the morning, straight after my shift. See what's up with the old bugger.

Clem was wailing now. The type you can't ignore.

OK. Jesus.

She changed and fed him and he fell into a quiet slumber. They spent the next half an hour cuddled up on the sofa in front of the TV and Sheila was nodding off when she heard a noise outside.

Clem started to scream.

Karen walked in all droopy eyed, lopsided grin. Stoned.

Without a word, Sheila passed Clem over and headed upstairs.

In her stained dressing gown, blonde hair coiled around her shoulders, peering through her bedroom window into the garden below where Karen was canoodling with Mike. She could tell by the sound of Karen's voice she was smitten with the useless lump.

She turned and scanned her bedroom. The half-full washing basket on the floor. The dusty exercise bike with a damp towel hanging over the handlebars. Box of nappies by the door. The bottles of pills lined up on her bedside table.

Aspirin. Clopidogrel. Cisoprolol. Ramipril. Her new best friends.

She would have to take the Aspirin and the Ramipril for the rest of her life. The prospect filled her with fret, as did the thought of the stent inside her, a tube of mesh squashing her 'fatty plaques', as the doctor called them. Fatty plaques!

She sat on the edge of the bed, undid her dressing gown and examined her body. She had been a yo-yo dieter over the years and had always found it easy enough to lose a stone but then put it right back on again. Problem was she was a mood eater.

Happy? Eat.

Sad? Eat.

Angry? Eat.

Bored? Eat.

Horny? Eat.

She pulled on a pair of tights, snapping the elastic, enjoying the feeling.

Clem was wailing in the room below. Karen's muffled shouts.

Mother of the year.

But everything was going to be OK—another month and Sheila would be out of here, starting a new life on the coast. She'd packed her bags so many times in her head she knew exactly what she'd take (not much). She was sick of the arguing, of being taken for granted. She'd been a doormat all her life—but no more.

Mind blank, she watched the second hand on her wall clock sweep through half a minute. She was due at work in a couple of hours—the joys of a waking night-shift.

Mam was in her usual spot on the settee, TV blaring. Eighty years old and deaf as a post. She tutted when Sheila came in and took the remote from the chair and muted the volume. Sheila examined the old lady tartan on Mam's legs, mottles of purple and cream.

How're your pins, Mam? Want me to check?

No need. Same as ever. Giving me gyp.

You remembering to use that cream?

With the sigh of a martyr, Mam straightened her top and brushed her purple nylon trousers. Her eyes were the palest grey and her hair was dyed the most shocking bright red colour.

Ronald McDonald, Sheila said.

Eh?

Cuppa?

Sheila headed to the kitchen while Mam nattered on. She took the mugs of tea through and sat in the chair beside her. They stared at the mute TV screen—a tank rocking on its caterpillar tracks, another war somewhere—supping their teas.

After a while, Mam said, Karen still knocking around with that fat apeth?

Aye.

Useless bag of shite.

He is that.

So how's your fella?

Eh?

Jake?

Whatever.

What's happened?

Nowt.

Doesn't sound like nowt. You sweet on him?

Don't talk daft.

Not what I've heard.

Oh aye, and what's that when it's at home?

Just that you're spending a lot of time with him in that blasted pub. More than's healthy like.

Rubbish. We're pals. Remember pals, Mam?

Edith's barely cold.

Mother!

Well think on. He's got sod-all cash if that's what you're after.

When Sheila didn't react, Mam added, You know Jake had a bairn?

He never talks about him.

Died when he was a youth. You not remember?

Told you, there's nowt going on between us.

If you say so.

Silence.

William, Mam said.

Eh?

His son. Playing football one day. Strapping lad. You sure you don't remember?

I'd say if I did.

Dropped dead just like that. Middle of a match.

Sheila checked the time and then got to her feet. I'll pop round tomorrow with the bairn.

Don't bother.

Why?

Don't want that little twat screaming the house down.

Nana of the year.

Leave him with Karen where he belongs, or it'll be your tit he's after before long.

Mam grinning her toothless grin.

Sheila got a taxi up to Dove Cottage the next morning and knocked on the front door. No reply. The curtains were closed but the bedroom window was open.

She called up: Jake?

She went around the back. The kitchen door was wide open. She moved along the corridor into the front room. Jake, sheathed in shadow, in his armchair beside the embers of the fire. It looked like he'd been there all night.

What you doing sitting in the dark?

She flung the curtains open and noticed the rifle propped in the corner of the room. His fierce gaze. The greasy stain on the antimacassar behind his head.

She went into the kitchen, took some eggs from the side and bacon from the fridge and poured some oil into the skillet. Lit the gas. The bread was stale. She stuck two slices in the toaster and took a plate and cutlery from the drying rack and went to pour a glass of milk but the milk was lumpy. Turning the bacon and egg in the skillet, examining her hands—did they always look this old? The toaster popped. She buttered the slices and dropped them onto the plate and got the ketchup and salt and pepper from the cupboard and positioned them in the centre of the table. Turned off the gas. Tipped the bacon and eggs onto the toast and placed the skillet in the sink.

Come on through, she shouted.

Footsteps. He looked at the table, looked at her. Sat. Started to eat. She poured him a glass of tap water and then cleaned the pots, studying the garden, the axe in the oak chopping block and a massive pile of logs. She turned, folded her arms, watching at him eat. His leg was jigging about. He kept glancing at something. She followed his gaze. The photograph of William on the mantelpiece.

Screech of swifts outside.

She sat beside him as he finished the last bit of egg. His hands and nails were acky.

He placed his knife and fork together and said, Thank you.

She nodded.

He turned the salt shaker slowly on the table top. Had a few off-days, he said.

I've been worried sick.

Sorry.

What you doing Saturday?

A shrug.

Fancy going for a walk? Bit of fresh? Blow the cobwebs away. Summat I need to talk to you about.

What?

Nowt that can't wait.

She pushed her chair back and got to her feet. He peered into her face. She cupped his chin, rubbing the bristle with her thumb.

He said, Can we go to the Ox?

I've just finished a night shift, apeth. Need to get some shut eye.

Right.

I'll see you Saturday, yeah? Come pick me up in the morning. We can go for a jar afterwards.

OK.

And get this ruddy house tided. It's a midden.

Home. She opened her laptop and checked her savings account. Just under £2,000. Then she double-clicked the calendar app.

Typed: *Hand notice in!*

Typed: *Move to Scarbados!*

She removed her clothes and climbed in between the cool bed sheets. A breeze chucked the curtain around, making the light swell and shrink in the room. A bird trilled nearby. A dog barked.

She thought about Jake again. Scarborough wasn't far. He could visit. She'd come back regular anyways. Might do him some good. Snap him out of it. Whatever 'it' was.

She rolled onto her side, knees raised, sliding her hands between her thighs, her thoughts spinning back to the rooms of her childhood, the bulky furniture, the paintings and rugs, the old dial telephone she wasn't allowed to use, the overgrown plants in the conservatory where her dad used to hide and drink and smoke. Dad's affairs, which, for many years, Mam pretended to be ignorant of.

Like her childhood belonged to someone else.

She climbed from the bed and pushed the window fully open. Heavy clouds scudded the horizon. A breeze moved fog through trees in the field opposite, tops flashing in the murk. She could smell the funk of her bedroom mixing with the air—metallic, watery. It filled her with a sense of longing to be far away from this dale.

THE MARL LAKE

Soon she heard the familiar rumble of Jake's quad bike. She shouldered her bag and opened the front door and they waved to each other as he pulled into the driveway. The neighbours across the road were sitting on deck chairs in their front garden rubbernecking.

She says, You right?

Champion.

Looking, sounding, more like himself again.

She tied her hair back and climbed on behind him and gripped the bars. He pulled through the estate at speed and steered them out of town towards Appersett, a place time forgot, where the villagers still hang their washing out on the village green. From here they climbed the steep, narrow roads into Cotterdale and parked on a gravel berm beside three vintage motorbikes.

Soon they reached the high watershed, an outcrop of humanoid rocks dominating the skyline. Below, the small lake held the pastel blue of the sky. Sheila was out of puff. She took the bottle of water from her bag, had a swig and passed it to him. She removed her cardigan and tied it around her waist and rubbed the sweat from her top lip.

He said, It's all downhill from here.

Story of my life. Look.

Above the brow of the hill a banana yellow para-glider was rising into the air, so close you could see the pilot's expression. Then a blue glider appeared and then a red one.

They must be mad, she said.

Sheila scanned the landscape, thinking about the conversation they needed to have. But he seemed all right, as if the past couple of weeks of ignoring her and being distant, never even happened.

He leaned into her, pointed, the heat of his skin against hers. That's Lovely Seat. And Pike Hill. And that over there, that's Bleak Haw. See? Where those hikers perished last winter. He stepped away from her.

I love it up here, she said. It's so wild.

Wild?

A-huh.

There's nowt wild about it. It's all man-made.

But it's nature, you know.

It's a desert. These hills are nowt but a sheep ranch. He kicked at something around his feet. See how short this ling is? And grass? Sheep. Mown to within an inch of its life. Listen.

Swatting flies from her face, she blinked at him.

Hear that?

What?

Exactly. Nowt. These hills should be covered in forest.

She scanned the landscape. I didn't realise.

Pricks that own the land, swiddening the moor, burning heather off to create new shoots for grouse to feed on. Reason yon dale floods. Peat acts like a sponge but when they burn it, they knacker it. All that

110

damage to folks' homes and businesses just so some posh southern twats can come up here once a year and shoot some game.

Thought you loved sheep.

That's not the point. There's nowt to get misty-eyed about with these here uplands. Whole of the North Country is the same. Ruined by sheep.

I think that's the most I've ever heard you say.

He cracked a half-smile. Howay.

They crossed the water sinks and Sheila leaned over the wall and glanced down into the diesel-coloured marl.

So how you getting on? Jake tapped his breastbone.

She shook her head. Some peace and flaming quiet would be nice.

I mean the rehab and whatnot?

Went to a couple of meetings.

And?

Wasn't my cup of tea. Saw a nutritionist at the outreach sessions. Gave me a diet plan.

It's working.

What?

You look thinner.

Does that mean I was enormous before?

He tutted. Women.

She opened her mouth.

He looked at her askance. What?

Nowt.

Wind blowing across the marl, smell of deep dark water. She peered towards the distant clinch of hillsides where the para-gliders reappeared for a second only to drop behind the dark crest of a hill. Structuring the sentence in her head, eventually she looked at him, her eyes drawn to the light caught in the hairs along his muscular forearms.

I'm moving.

Where?

Scarborough.

He looked pale, drawn.

The cardiac proper scared me. What's it called? Moment of clarity. Muggins here, realised they're all using me. Don't feel like I've got a frigging life any more. Just need to get away for a while. A break. Scarborough's not far. You can visit. Always fancied the coast. Walking along the beach every day. Do me a world of good. Don't you think?

He wouldn't meet her eye.

It's the only way I'll ever get shot of them. Mam, Karen, Bear, that blasted kid. Whoever said being a grandparent was like eating all the chocolate you want and never getting fat was talking out of their jacksy.

He nodded once, cleared his throat.

You're the only person I've told. Apart from my boss. Karen's wanting to move in with Mike. She's there most of the time anyway. And I've got a care job sorted. Somewhere to lodge until I find a little flat. It's—

The words run out.

Jake looked like he was about to share a thought, but then he reached out and grabbed her arms, pulling her into him. He began to move, side-stepping, his singing deep, haunting, pure:

My dear, it rains, it hails, it snows,
And I am wet unto my clothes,
And I pray you let me in,
And I pray you let me in...

She was moving with him, twisting with happiness, sensing the blood whirling hot within them both.

Oh no, kind sir, that never can be,
For there's no one in the house but me,
And I cannot let you in,
And I cannot let you in...

112

As if he understood the mystery of living within her skin. As if this was all he needed to do, in this moment, to make what she had just said disappear. But then he let go of her, releasing her from the dream of him. The moment was lost.

Sorry, he said, and walked away.

SHEILA'S PLACE

Lumps of springs in the bare mattress. Stains on the carpet. Marks on the walls and headboard. They were a postcard from her past: wish you weren't here. Soon home-time children would fill the estate with life and it will mean it is time to leave. She tried not to think whether it was right or wrong leaving like this, what life would be like away from this house, this estate, these familiar things.

She moved over to the window and pressed her forehead against the cool glass. Wind-blown raindrops sashayed in runnels down the pane. She eyed the house opposite.

Mr Kennedy's Irish granddaughters used to visit during the summer holidays, coming over on the ferry every year, and Karen would play with them in the fields down by the old railway line. It seemed like such a long time ago now, the kids in the backfields, Karen still a sweet-natured girl. Before she hit puberty and it was all sulks and flares of anger. Problem was she never grew out of it.

Sheila sat on the mattress and removed her purse from her handbag and looked at the small photograph inside. A bar in Greece, candles and music and sweet drunken chaos, Bear's lips pulled tight with that raucous laughter of his, laughter that made her veins fizz.

But here he is invading her thoughts again: Jake. That mad embrace by the lakeside, that queer slow-dance. *And I cannot let you in*. What did it mean? Please stay? Don't go? Or: Thank you. I'll miss you. Some kind of premonition? Either way, he'd stopped answering her texts. But she'd be back to the Dales soon enough, weekend visits, days off. Christmas wasn't far away. She'd go see him at the cottage or meet him in the Ox for a few jars. I'll write to him, she thought, but then, for some reason, her thoughts turned to her dad in his hospital bed. How small he looked. The smell of his skin, the nicotine on his yellowy fingers, the scalpy smell of his bald head as she kissed it. How she could sense the rot between her parents setting in. How Mam began to mimic that louring tone towards him, a tone Sheila had learned to accept as part of her dad's affection. But mostly she thought about his final words: Take care of your mam, you're all she's got. But it didn't feel like it after he passed away, the house full of men's grunts and smells and shady morning-looks.

Things were going to be different now. Sheila's life wasn't going to be a life less-lived, a life lived for others. She was leaving for a not-so-faraway yet-to-be. It was the most selfish thing she had ever done and it felt...

How did it feel?

She wasn't sure. She just couldn't be doing with the drama of telling them. They'd kick up a fuss and she'd only end up staying and hating herself even more. It just wasn't an option.

Mam's voice in her head: You're a selfish cow.

Sheila's eyes fell shut.

She recalled her trip to Scarborough last February, wandering alone along the dark and blustery streets down to the Spa House, watching starlings around the cliff-face, flocks melding like smoke.

Something in her stomach was telling her not to leave. Some deep gut-burn saying this was the wrong decision.

Nerves, she told herself. Ignore it.

The peals of children's laughter trickled into the room. She checked her watch. The taxi would be here any minute. She watched her suitcase on the other side of the room as if it was conscious, as if it would tell her something.

Go. Stay.

She lugged the suitcase downstairs. The house was silent. She went to the kitchen window and rubbed the dusty leaves of the jade plant Jake had given her.

Like putting a fingernail in soil and growing a whole new person.

She snapped off a branch, unzipped her suitcase and shoved it inside.

Bleep of a text. Thrum of an engine outside.

Time. Nowt left to do now but go.

She straightened the chairs beneath the kitchen table and placed her coffee cup in the sink. On the surface of the coffee floated a bluebottle. She stared at the dead fly remembering the last meal they shared together as a family. The last silly argument they had. Just remembering.

Present day

KIRK DALE

Woken by low-flying exercises through the hills all afternoon, jets booming overhead. He pinches the blood and warmth back into his limbs and then makes his way across the dusky in-bye land. Huddles of pheasants. Parallel lines of iced-over sieves and tractor tracks. Some of the land back in sown cereals, wheat and barley and rape. Clashy lowland after potatoes, fields of weedy set-aside. He takes the landscape in as one continuous thing because eventually you become the farm and the farm becomes you.

Along this ancient pathway, outstriding his fear, the rifle over his shoulder, following the National Park path across the fields and sheep trods to Howl Dale, making progress now, navigating by the stars, examining the composition of the night. The cold stings his face. So many obstacles to negotiate, electric fences, squeeze stiles, thorn dykes, frozen mole heaves. Take you a fortnight to get home at this bastard rate. Up through a hagg and into the fields again, the icy wind on his sweat chilling him. Accepting the fact that he isn't as fit as he thought. But he begins to enjoy the pace. Chewing at something stuck in his teeth, looking to his south across the Vale of Pickering and hills of the Wolds, the occasional flash of an orange light. Gritter truck.

January on the land when there seemed to be all the time in the world but then it was all rush, rush, rush. It was the month of laying hedges, maintaining fences and gates, clearing ditches, cleaning out stock sheds and spreading muck. Battling with frozen water supplies. Feeding and bedding livestock. Strip grazing. Fattening sheep on swedes and kale. Sorting hodded potatoes and carrots and bagging the last of the sugar beet to be sent to the factory.

Moving on towards Little Edge Woods and Pickering Beck, the chill evening air watered his nose and eyes. Sixty-five miles, he tells himself. Following the beck upstream he crosses a wooden footbridge and skirts the northern edge of the town, so close he can make out the creamy light coming from late-night windows. Feeding on the loneliness, the dark, the chill. Don't turn inwards. To the west of Kirkbymoorside he drops down into Thin Oak's Wood and Kirk Dale. Sixty miles. Can't be much more.

I will sing of a place that is dear to my heart,
A place where I always would dwell,
And if you will kindly lend me an ear
A few of its beauties I'll tell…

The amount of times he's driven that road on his way to a new job or over to the seaside with Edith and William, never imagining he would be walking through this land on a midwinter's night, seventy-three years old trying to get back home.

Happen he could just stick out his thumb? Not everyone pays heed to the TV news or reads the papers any more. Order a taxi? Back home in a couple of hours.

Apeth.

He pictures himself walking down off Jackdaw Moor and into the back garden. He knows they'll be watching the cottage. Knows this. But he imagines himself kicking the snow from his boots and closing the kitchen door behind him. His heart twinkling at the intimate smell of the cottage—the smell of Edith's scalp. Calling out her name. She will respond with footsteps and the waft of hairspray and cinnamon. He sees himself climbing into his grief bed, her dress spread out next to him. Just to be home and sit where he usually sits, quiet beside the dip in the cushions. The hollow she left behind. To listen and settle in. Drinking tea, discuss their gripes.

Let me go.

Then the police can have him, do what they want. Because the cuffs they will clasp around his wrist will be no different to the watch he wore for years keeping him a prisoner to time, making money for other men. This is what he thinks about as he drives one aching foot in front of the other, aware of the lunge and pull of his muscles, the land about him hushed, the quarter moon sinking with its metallic glaze.

For it brings me back those happy times when roaming free and wild,
I played about my native home,
I played about my native home,
I played about my native home,
A merry mountain child.

Be daylight soon. He's made slow-progress. He fills his water bladder in the beck and then makes a den in the protective shelter of a dirt hole, a flood-cut bank beneath the vast root system of an ancient oak.

The following evening, rifle in his hands, he makes his way to the edge of a hagg, muttering to himself. The low dark blanket of sky tells him rain or snow is coming in maybe two or three hours, but the strong smell of the trees suggests sooner. He picks some Wood Ear fungi from an elder tree and some cleavers and sorrel. Chewing, scanning the blue-black land. He is about to set off again when something makes him pause, listen. Heart pulsing, raising a quick sweat, he shoulders the rifle. His breathing has a hitch to it. He leans against the bole of a tree, steadying himself. Is someone there?

Ahead, the land. Behind him, barren woodland. Both quiet.

But he saw them earlier: fresh foils that weren't his own.

After a while he lowers the rifle, squinting into the occlusion of tree limbs. A quick mental reconnoitre. Crack in the undergrowth.

Show yourself! Jake calls.

Silence.

Jake slips a round into the air.

A rustle. Jake locates the direction and takes a step forward, rifle shouldered, ready to slip the trigger. Dark figure running between the trees. Glint of something. A weapon? He lets off a couple of warning shots, tucks the rifle under his arm and launches himself onto the dusky land, trotting like a man twenty years his junior, committing himself to the unknown.

Disembodied voices creep across the moonlit landscape. He feels surrounded by shadows in the dark, like he's a moat of ill-luck. Squatting behind hedges whenever he sees headlights on the A170. Aiming the rifle into the dark nothingness. Watching, waiting. Metallic taste of adrenalin in his throat, the sweat on his back turning a dreadful cold. Snowflakes flit among his whispers.

"What is that blood on thy shirt sleeve?
My son, come tell it unto me."
"'Tis the blood of my dear brother,
Who I killed under yonder tree."

There: a vehicle pulling into the side of the road. He crouches low, holding the rifle by the fore-stock, lowering his face, lips moving as if in prayer.

Soon he is on the outskirts of Helmsley and knows he is being followed. He crosses the narrow Carlton Road towards the final house out of town. At the entrance, a hand scythe is lodged into the top of a gatepost. A beat-up motorbike in the driveway. Grass and weeds growing high. No lights on inside the house. He spots the three series Land Rover, similar to one he had back in the 1970s. He always had problems with the stop solenoid and lift pump but he knew that Haynes manual like a priest knows his pencil-marked scripture.

Steering the Land Rover along the A170 at speed. Slow down. Think. He decides to take the less obvious route south through Sproxton and Ampleforth, the car stinking of damp and adrenalin, an eggy smell coming from the heater. Amid scrappy woodland, the loud crackle of tyres gripping the salt on the road. Headlights in his rear-view, distant.

Lip told them, he has to take you out. Has to be him. They know you're armed. He's going to say it was self-defence. Need to hand yourself in. No. Tomorrow. One more night in your own bed. Be back in what, an hour? You'll get caught. Police station in Thirsk won't be open. Ripon? No. Haven't seen any police. Not all this time. Just the whump of a helicopter. Searching the forest and coast, that's probably why. Useless. Watching the dark trees passing by as if only vaguely aware of the proceedings. Eyeing the rear-view, the car that was trailing him appears to have gone. The TV, they don't know what to make of you, saving the lass from the sea, like they can't—

Sudden, his boots shamble the pedals, vehicle coming to a skidding halt. Blaze of lights on the road ahead, irregular arrangements of quads and 4x4s. Roadblock. Jake absorbs the scene in an instant: the sudden ugliness of what awaits. He switches off the headlights and reverses at speed, up the lane and into a field, spinning the vehicle around. Along a pot-holed drive, dark outbuildings coming into view, he cuts the engine and freewheels down between gateposts and out into an open field, leaning towards the windscreen squinting.

Fuck.

He pumps the brakes, eyes adjusting to the dark—thirty, forty metres away: shapes approaching.

Grabbing the pack to shield himself, he slides out of the vehicle and dashes towards the trees. He runs straight into a barbed wire fence, stumbling onto his knees, struggling to his feet in the glare of the approaching headlights. Righting himself against a tree trunk, he keeps moving with the sound of engines behind him—

But then he is falling.

A muzzle-flash. Jake holds his breath. Shadows, lights, voices, a dog's bark. Lodged between the bankside and a prone tree, dirt and leaf fall and small rocks cover him. Torchlights moving among the branches. The sound of water nearby, stench of wet earth. The backpack next to him. He feels for the zip and the hunting knife, his knuckles brushing wet bark. You're OK. It feels like a long time passes and he is sure the men are almost on top of him. The electric blaze of everything they are going to do to him. Waiting for certain death. Then all is quiet, dark.

Rolling onto his side, needles of pain shoot through his thighs, rendering him with miserable pangs. Rocking with exertion, shuffling onto his feet until he is facing the slope he came down, he pulls himself out and pisses onto his wounds. Then he staggers over to the backpack and removes the Ruger, checking for damage.

Half an hour later he knows exactly where he is. Elm Hag, just to the west of Byland Abbey. Above him, the deep northern sky is a metropolis of starlight—reminding him of the passage ahead. Can't be more than forty miles away from home now. Maybe less. His body shivers. Harried in his mind by the men tracking him, he is minutely conscious of each footstep. Blood turning cold around his knees, he lopes across the road into a field where ploughed earth cords the land. Down into a wooded ghyll, stumbling into a spiny thicket of blackthorn, tearing the arm of his parka clean open. Following the beck downstream, moving slowly through the skeletons of the trees, tilting his face up to where the sky shimmers, speckles of snow landing on his face. He bears westwards. Not enough light for moon-shadows but ample to see by. Casting his eyes about the constellations again when it hits him: no memory of this land. None. But the men are out there somewhere, circling. Or maybe not. He's not entirely convinced it occurred.

> I said, 'My lovely creature, come tell me where you dwell.'
> 'Beside the bonny hawthorn that blooms in the dale,
> That blooms in the dale,
> That blooms in the dale,
> Beside the bonny hawthorn that blooms in the dale.'

After an hour he thinks he sees the blue lights of a distant patrol car but that doesn't make sense. Then he sees it again—streetlights of villages and towns far below him. He is on top of the inland cliff of Sutton Bank. He takes the binoculars from his pack and glasses the country far below—the table-land of the Vale of Mowbray. He's halfway home.

Following the steep track down through the trees to the empty car park, he pauses to admire the enormous lime figure carved into the hillside, the white horse glowing in the dark.

He reaches the village outskirts as morning breaks and finds himself at the back of a garden so large he can't see the house it surrounds. Snagging his way through a blackthorn bush, sneaking through the gate silent as a shadow towards a ramshackle shed, he peers through the window and then slides the stiff hasp and pushes the door open. He removes his pack and locates the gaffa tape and patches the rip in his parka arm. Then he lifts one of the deck chairs from the wall, unfolds it and sits down. Exploring the wounds on his legs, bringing his fingers to his lips. Taste of rust.

The following dawn he reaches the main road beneath the A1. Studying the scene, a couple of lorries rumble overhead. Under the flyover a car passes him from behind, headlights striping him. Nowt to say they noticed. Quickly he is back into the fields and the growing cold. He realises where he is and where he can spend the daylight hours, across the fields around Kirklington towards the Camp Hill Estate, making his way into the gloomy woodland as daylight comes across the land.

There: he spots one. He removes the rifle and stalks his way into the trees nice and easy, concealing his approach, locking onto the squirrel as it scampers up the trunk. He makes a squeaking noise at the side of his mouth. The squirrel freezes, flicking its tail. Jake slips the trigger. The squirrel goes down. Then a rasping behind him, another one showing face. He settles the crosshairs.

> *A squirrel is a funny bod,*
> *'E wears a bushy tail,*
> *Ya day 'e teeuk awd Grimy's coat*
> *An' hung it on a rail.*

Close of day, stooped against the wind, toiling up Masham Lane, he realises he is still two nights' walk from home. The fear of the men stalking him. This abrupt craving for a pint of dark ale and three fingers of whiskey beside a warm hearth. The effort helps put it from his mind, concentrating on his step, stopping every ten metres to catch his wind, admiring the slopes of the low hills around him, blue in the moonlight. Thinking about William glissading down the fells as a lad, his legs in a fertiliser bag, and then home for tea, his fingers cold-swollen. Going back two winters, coming inside after an afternoon in the garden and here's Edith staring blankly out of the window. He talks to her, places a hand on her arm but she continues to gawp as if he isn't even there.

Beginning to change, going the way she went, doing her toilet in strange places, picking her up when she'd fallen. Dr Phillips, the family doctor, formal in his blue suit and plain brown tie, loosening her nightie with his bony hands. His face—those piercing, rheumy eyes—appearing so malevolent in the space above her.

That sound.

Sirens. The whump of a helicopter's rotor blades.

He waits, eyeing the sky.

Howay.

Down into the ghyll, the snow not so deep here, just patches among the trees, the crunch of frozen leaf-mulch beneath his boots as he crosses the wooden footbridge connecting the island near South Spring, following the way-signs towards the woods of Ellington Firth. Making good progress, stopping briefly to scan the sky, a wind getting up, honeycombed flakes falling from branches. He examines the ground behind him, fresh snowfall covering his foils.

Smell of bacon in the morning, rabbit and onion in the evening. Tinkering with engines in the yard, avoiding her. Spending the afternoon in the garden greening his fingers, clearing the flower beds, sowing seeds or tinkering with the water butt until she calls him inside to the smell of baking, singing along to the radio, the lad on his belly in front of the TV drawing, the collie asleep on the rug next to him.

William was always drawing them when he was a bairn, usually in the living room together watching TV. So many pictures of them on the walls. Falling asleep with his crayons, colours melting in his chubby hands.

Then in the kitchen before bedtime, making bait for the next day, beef and mustard on white, something from the garden, a salt shaker and hard-boiled egg. Morning it's the flask of tea and gathering the knapsack and the puckered peck over the threshold.

On, slow but sure, a lone figure moving between the internal paths and open canopies of the Firth, walking for so long with such heavy steps, but other than his memories nowt made much of an impression any more. Roaming back to when he first met her—never so much future in his life as in that moment. Even towards the end he always saw the younger her, the knockout beauty he met at the factory gates. Those cute dimples and sleepy wide-set eyes—eyes so blue they hurt to look at, like she was lit from the inside. She thought her size eight feet were manly and made fun of herself a lot. She was genuinely caring but hated sentimentality almost as much as her middle name, and he'd call her Felicity whenever he wanted to tease her out of a mood. She loved a real fire and being out in the garden during a storm and singing and dancing along to the radio. Walking behind her just to see her neck, her hair usually done up in a chignon, those dark hairs in a V pointing down her spine. Winter wrapped in furs, everyone turning to look. Other women on the line called her a stuck-up cow. Ten years his senior. Toy boy, eh. Wondering why me? She wasn't a woman's woman. Happen this should've told him summat. Dwindling under her confidence and beauty like some power held over him. That it took someone like her to shape the little there was of his mind, yield to her. But did being true to her mean he had no will of his own?

He saw the journey of their love right up to that morning just over a year ago when he found her in bed beside him, her face slack, a gawp. Flower? Climbing out of bed and stepping over to the window, the moor outside anchoring low cloud—the world didn't look any different but it should have. Stepping back over to her, his scalp prickling, kissing her cheek, sliding his hand under her shoulder.

What did you go and do that for?

Pulling her close, squeezing her. A rattle in her chest like she was trying to speak.

A blessing, maybe, dying in her sleep. Unlike William, dying in fear.

But there are no farewells in death.

The week following, folk coming to the cottage to offer platitudes, as if they wanted to share in his pain, but he just wanted them to go away because it wasn't something inside him, it was an ache in the world and they were only adding to it.

The months went by and he felt the tension slackening, as if she was stitched into him and he was unpicking the threads—doing me, undoing me. Amazed by how much he loved her still.

Just one last chance to utter those three words:

I forgive you.

PENHILL

He pauses in the middle of the dark paddock, thinking. Almost 1 am. The surrounding land is quiet, still. The ground outside the field shelter is poached. He'd spent the day hiding out in the Abbey grounds, leaving it as late as he could before he made a move. But there is no house in sight, just the main road to worry about and that's usually dead.

The three horses turn to look at him as he enters, hoving about in their matching grey winter rugs, ears pricked and twitching. Talking quietly to them, waiting for them to settle, he examines the interior of the shelter. Hay-nets split around the walls. Buckets of iced-over water sitting in tyres. Head collars and coils of sail line hanging from snecks.

He is drawn instantly to the small bay mare. Broad-backed and calm, she seems amiable, which is good because the other is a bargy-looking cob and the other maybe a half thoroughbred, way too big and probably feisty. He takes what he doesn't need from his backpack and stacks it outside the shelter, surprised by how light the pack is when he shoulders it on. He breaks the ice in the buckets with the rifle's stock.

Owd Jim Slack 'e 'ad a grey 'oss,
such an 'oss as you never did see...

Unhooking a head collar and a line rope, he approaches the mare singing gently to her, sliding his hand beneath the rug to rub her flank. She blinks at him, licking her chin. He's always loved their sweet musky smell. He checks her hooves for shoes, relieved she's barefoot. It will keep the snow from balling up. He undoes the buckle on the head collar and slides it over her nose, pulling the strap around her head and fastening it. Then he fashions a rein with the sail line, thinking: Am I just making a noose? He checks the rug straps are tight and gathers some hay and stuffs it into his backpack to feed her with later. Then he leads her out into the paddock not expecting the other two horses to follow but here they are. The mare seems hesitant and keeps looking back at them. Jake clicks his tongue at her. He locks them behind the gate and mounts her. The horses whinny from behind the fence and the mare nickers in response.

Wi' a lump on 'is rump an' 'is owd tail stump,
an' 'is legs bent aht an' blinnd in one e'e...

Twisting her into the spool of night, the track bending north up Stark Bank, negotiating the salt and sludge and patches of ice, the scabs on his thighs fragmenting. Up onto the exposed moor road and into a rapid change of weather, snow drifting across the bridleway, peppering his face. The mare quickens her step, lifting her head, ears twisting, her rug warm beneath him. He falls to a coughing fit and she looks back at him as if studying his face. He slaps her neck. Good lass. Soon they are making their descent towards Melmerby, the mare clouting her way through the deeper drifts, and he recalls a scene from over a decade ago, seeing a rake of young studs being released into a paddock flank-deep with snow, gambolling and bucking like spring lambs.

Urging her on with his heels. He blinks at the stars above, scattering like gooseflesh through the night. In a swap of wind, he hears the nearby trees moving. Holds his breath. Nowt. Pointing her north, after a hundred metres they come to a wooden fence and walk it some distance before he has to dismount, feeling the burn of muscle in his legs and back from riding. He opens the gate, the hasp clattering, making his heart pulse. He climbs the fence and pulls her nearer and remounts. They pass through the wickerwork of trees and out the other side, heading into the high country. By the time they cross the main road he realises he hasn't seen a single set of headlights for over an hour and the only foils he's seen are of his own making. The moon is high, illuminating skifts of snow drifted against the drystone walls. Touching the rifle at his shoulder, reassuring. A fingerpost leads onto the moor road hidden by snow. She loses her footing a few times and side-steps but keeps on. Solid, reliable.

I'll ride him to the huntsman,
So freely I will give
My body to the hounds then,
I'd rather die than live.
Poor owd horse, poor owd horse...

Soon they come to a cattle grid and he dismounts again and leads her through the bypass gate. Scraping the snow from his boots, he climbs a couple of the fence slats and remounts, embracing the rug around her shoulders for warmth.

It has been following him all the way up here, a light-headed sensation that skews his vision and makes his blood pump feebly. As they reach the high plateau, the sides of the road deep with ploughed snow, his arms and hands and legs are beginning to lose their strength.

Penhill, summit plateau with its cairns lost in the dark and snow flurries. On the flank of the hillside the snow pauses, pale cusp of moon flashing through the cloud. He pulls the reins and they stand a while in the chill, the break in weather revealing the vast Vale below, towns and villages to the north-east. Bedale. Northallerton. Stretching over to Middlesbrough and Redcar and the North Sea.

Where's Lip and his men?

He has to find a place to leave the mare before daylight breaks or he might as well have a target on his back. Then he'll hide the day away and set off at dusk and be home by midnight. Smiling briefly, a boy fulfilling a dream, he pats her neck, speaking to her. Slow and steady they move down the road between the snow-drifted fences and drystone walls. Turning her left near the training gallops, a solitary light down in West Witton, following the rim of the fell, the road leads down between the smell of cattle in the snow-covered pastures, onto High Lane bridleway where the ground levels off, the surface frozen to a crust, crisp sounds beneath her hooves.

Later. The mare drinks from the part-frozen beck. Her flanks are beginning to heave. She needs to rest. Rifle across his lap, he studies the rise of land. Be light soon. She raises her head and shakes it about, something stuck to her nose. He clicks his tongue and orders her to walk on, crossing a small humpbacked bridge slow and careful, breaking pockets of ice. Studying the blue wet light spreading upwards in the east. He spots the farmhouse over to his left, a metal trough at the field-edge. He dismounts and walks her through the gate and over to the trough, breaking the ice with the rifle's stock. The farmer will find her soon enough. She'll be fine. He pulls the handful of hay from his backpack and leaves it in a pile on the snow.

Now 'e teeak 'er some 'ay all iv a scuttle,
'Er poor awd belly began ti ruttle...

He rubs her muzzle.

Thank you.

He heads off, watching the landscape colour up. Soon he comes to a frozen cascade and then a little wooden bridge leading onto the fell. Picturing himself gyring up Carperby Sleights, following The Straights west onto Jackdaw Moor and Dove Cottage. He knows he should find somewhere to camp but with the proximity of home pressing in on him he continues. Waiting for a motorbike to pass on the A684, he crosses the salt and sludge into a flurry of snow coming slantwise. Then he spots a pair of headlights jouncing across the higher land, churning the snow, a 4x4 with gun-mounted beams and a bar across the driver's side—a lamping set-up.

Dark figure inside, leaning towards the windscreen.

Jake drops to his knees, unlimbs the backpack and drops it into the snow. He removes the spare magazine and the hunting knife and shuffles over to the drystone wall, raising himself up, resting the barrel on a coping stone because his hands tremble so.

He scopes the landscape. Nowt but snow.

Then he spots the man moving closer, halting between the V of trunks on a coppiced oak. Jake ducks behind the wall to the corkscrew buzz of two bullets overhead, reports caroming around the hillsides, scaring birds from their roosts.

He finds a missing stone in the wall and inserts the barrel. Lowering his eye to the scope he is unprepared for what he sees: Lip Monroe's face in the crosshairs, a grin like an axe wound, a look Jake can't intuit because he isn't seeing Lip's face he is seeing William's, not a semblance but an echo, the perfect stamp of features.

That small photo in Charles' room at the nursing home—was it William or was it Lip? Did Jake get it wrong?

He calculates the distance, speed. Slips the trigger. But Lip has gone.

He turns and lopes across the snowy incline, gritting his teeth, certain he is safe, but the first bullet tears into his left arm, making him spin around, and the second is like a punch, rig-welting him into the snow.

Nine weeks earlier

THE PARK

That night a storm hurried in. A pattern had emerged over the past couple of weeks: two fine days followed by a closeness in the dale, fat clouds pressing down and the seizure of electrical nights, only to be blown away by winds the following morning, bringing the smell of hay being cut and summer-end birdsong. 'Fremd' the old farmers used to call it—Viking on their tongues. Tonight, it was whipping up static charge, lightning taking on tensile energy and pulling moonlight from the sky, twisting Jake deeper into himself than he'd ever been before.

He gathered his things and filled his hipflask with whiskey, scratching at the pewter's patina with his long fingernails, thinking. Then he placed the rifle in its case, slung it across his shoulder and headed to the quad.

Alone in the shank of the night, feeling so on edge, his senses alive to him, standing in the centre of the park eyeing the dark shapes of the sycamore trees where earlier he'd seen the knots of corvids coming in to roost, shadows against the lens of the moon.

He was experiencing emotions he didn't have names for.

It was the spot where William died, playing football with his mates that Sunday morning. Jake was in the pub when he got the news. Edith was visiting a pal in Askrigg. They arrived at the hospital at the same time. William passed away just moments before. Their quiet, sweet-natured, orange-eyed angel. He would have grown into such a beautiful man.

Rumbles of thunder bouncing around the hills. Lightning dancing in the west.

Folks died. That's how it was. Some in their sleep or by disease or accident. Some by their own hand.

Pulling his cap down, beads of water soaking his collar and cuffs, moonlight shredded the clouds, and through the raindrops beading his eyelashes it was as if he was seeing stars for the first time—unexpected constellations.

He moved over to the shelter of a sycamore and unzipped the rifle case, lifting the stock to his shoulder, aiming at the spot where William fell.

Seeing Sheila in the hospital a few weeks ago—how it brought it all back, the journey home from the hospital, Edith beside him in the car but she was a mirror. Losing a child, it crawls down your throat and eats you alive. Jake didn't know who he was any more, a stranger to himself living in a stranger's house and there was no way he could ever get home again and find it was all a dream, enter the living room and find Edith and William sitting in front of the TV together.

After William's death a hush descended on the cottage, but a quietude that could never be mistaken for tranquillity, because even as the days turned into weeks and the pain transformed into something you just can't bear to live with, one thing that never melted away was the feeling that they were each to blame—for not being there when he died, for not getting to the hospital sooner, for not knowing about his faulty heart.

Edith took it upon herself to make the front room hers. She moved her favourite green wing-back chair in there and the radio and all of her gubbins. Humming along to the light programmes while she embroidered tray-cloths or cardigans or bits for the expectant mams in town, bootees and matinee jackets and hats, completely unaware of how uncomfortable it made them feel. She even knitted a gansey for Jake, a triple wave. Encouraging him to do what? Set sail? Be off? Then she took to sleeping in William's bed and Jake considered putting a lock on the door. It was as if her relationship with William had been separate from his, that they had been living different lives.

He said, I didn't think I could feel more saddened than I do, but—

But what?

You must know it hurts. You can't even look me in the eye.

She looked startled. Jake.

What?

She pointed at the fireplace as a bird dropped onto the hearth. It flapped around and then took flight, smashing into the windowpane with such force Edith yelped. A raven, huddle of feather, beak, claw, readying to attack. Edith ran from the room. Jake opened the window and stepped back. The bird eyed him, shook its feathers, hopped along the windowsill and flew away.

No more beauty in the world. Such little love but he took what he could and was thankful. The years of drinking that followed, a kind of ceremony.

With moonlight glissing off the barrel, Jake slipped the trigger, a crisp let off. Birds battered through the canopy, caws inarticulate, like the roar of a crowd at a football match.

Inhaling the nitro from the rifle, he unbuttoned his coat and placed his hand against his chest. Faint flutter beneath his ribcage. He closed his eyes to make the memories go away.

Glisten of rhododendron, epitaphs flickering, swirls of a Celtic cross beneath a blowsy yew tree. That familiar path. Here she is. He crouched, running his fingertips into the rain-worn words. *Edith Felicity Eisner.* Turned, peering through the darkness towards him. Our sweet lad. Touching his forehead against the cold stone, he pushed his fingers into the soil, and between finger and thumb, he pinched some of the moist earth and placed it onto his tongue.

He received a postcard from Sheila the following week. The picture on the front showed Scarborough's South Bay and the distant Oliver's Mount taken from a high vantage point. Not much of a message on the back, just her new address and phone number. *Hope you're keeping well. I often think of you. Come visit!*

He held the postcard to his neb. Sniffed.

Escaping the needy druggy daughter and forever griping bairn. Better for her health, her heart. He knew this. But at times he missed her. Wished she would pop in. The boozy afternoons in the Ox, the meals at hers. He should have answered the door when she came to say goodbye, shouting through the letterbox. I'll write to her, he thought, propping the postcard on the mantelpiece next to the photograph of William.

Later. He finished his lunch, scraped his plate off into the fire and watched it shuffle on the coals. The next few minutes, still and silent, memories flooded the room. Edith's third trimester, lying awake at night watching her, listening to her moans and gibberish, moonlight illuminating her bump, the baby influencing her dreams. Seeing her carry another man's child, how alone he felt, like an interloper in bed beside her, beside them. She now belonged to society in a way he never would, moving through that glass wall from being a woman to a mother. Jake observing her as if from a great distance. The way the townsfolk changed towards her. Women wanting to touch her all the time. It felt like they were all laughing in his face.

Then in bed one night she turned to him, opened her eyes and smiled, as if she sensed he had been watching. She took his hand and placed it on her stomach and he felt it kick and kick again. For the first time it became real, a real little body pressing at the edges of its underwater world. Jake no longer felt so abandoned. Because infertility is a lonely kind of death.

Then it was as if Edith's mam had become her Siamese twin, and then the midwife was there all the time too, the house full of women, it seemed. Then all that nonsense about a drug-free birth. It made Jake chuckle. Trying to describe the birthing process to Edith as cautiously— and then with the smell of blood and internal organs in his mind— as bluntly as he could. Anyway, two hours into labour and she was screaming out for gas and air. The way it comes, the explosion of new life in the house. This new-born alien creature. Watching her holding William as a baby. She caught Jake observing her more than once.

His days felt twisted, time began to fray. The temperature was beginning to drop as if the season were reflecting his mood, peeling back, deepening—warm rainy days bleeding into the sharp brilliant skies of early autumn.

The TV and radio were on day and night, something like company. He spent hours beside the hearth warming his bones. He slept whenever he wanted to sleep but never managed more than a couple of hours. Curtains closed, eyes falling on the rifle propped in the corner of the room. He hadn't dressed or stepped outside for days. His beard was longer, softer. He kept stroking it.

Often he found himself standing outside William's bedroom door, a hand on the doorknob, feeling like he couldn't breathe. Like he was out in the park again in the gathering storm, a dark figure melding with the shadows of the sycamores, raindrops falling from a thousand hand-shaped leaves, feeling something inarticulate, something filled with so much blame it was incomprehensible.

Edith?

Next week was the anniversary of her death.

Those final days when he just sat with her, reading her romance novels to her. Pausing, listening, eyeing her chest. Was she breathing? Wishing William was alive to help shoulder the burden. The wall of his resolve being removed stone by stone.

Pre-dawn he rose up on his elbows: the bedroom door being inched to. Footsteps along a distant hallway. Wrinkles in the fabric of time.

He went down into the living room and stood amid the quiet mess of the place.

You there?

Dawn light filled the house—liquid, turbid, mineral.

Midday he ate a piece of toast and drank some tea and went upstairs. For the first time in years, he entered the time capsule, the mausoleum of William's room. Things unmoved. Dust. Wanting to refold you, insert you back into me. Heart. Brain. Blood. Bone.

Just things. Not him. Not our sweet lad.

Later still. He awoke on William's bed aware of his heart racing. He made his way into the bathroom to piss. Then he washed his face and placed his comb under the tap, running it through his hair and beard, smiling at himself, eyes bloodshot—red as the harvest moon outside. Thick wedge of tangled beard, fine red delta on his forehead and cheeks, tonsure of silver hair sticking up.

Even though he was almost ten years her junior, he was the first to turn grey. Badger, she called him. And it wasn't the gradualness of turning grey that struck him, or how it altered his looks, but rather the silence of it, of a change so dramatic from his almost jet-black hair to a platinum silver. He felt it should have made a noise: the turning of a screw, the creak of a rusty hinge.

He picked up the soap dish and smashed it into the mirror.

Night. A figure in the garden below—Father chopping firewood in his vest and braccs, sweating in the moonlight. The memory of the segs on his palms like coins. Father straightening his back, rubbing sweat from his brow. He threw a quick glance at Jake, a scowl of disappointment— always that look. *You let that rich cunt fuck your wife and you did nowt?* Father swung the maul high, bringing it down dead centre of the log, moonlight glinting off the blade.

Late afternoon, riding the bald moor to the thorpe of Wappentake, to the care home where Charles Monroe resided. Pulling into a parking space, engine puttering through his thighs, Jake eyed the porticoes around the doorway, the leaded lancet windows. Dusk drawing near.

You can do this.

Behind the glass of the front door: a grey-haired woman with a metal cane. She stared at him as he rang the bell.

He signed in at the reception desk with another man's name.

All easy smiles and tinkles of laughter, a nurse led him down the gravy-smelling hallway. Jake paused outside the TV room. Elderly folks in robes and slippers asleep in their chairs or staring into space. I'd rather be dead. The nurse ahead of him, knocking on a door.

Large high-ceilinged room, smell of cleaning fluids.

Jake looked everywhere but directly at Charles.

Charles, the nurse said. Someone here to see you. She sounded forlorn, and the way she smiled at Jake as she left the two men alone.

Jake moved to the far side of the room. He couldn't bring himself to look. Not yet. Touching the objects on the sideboard. A silver tray. Shoe horn. Cuticle press. He lifted a small mirror, rust spotted with age, tilting it so he could see the reflection of Charles behind him, upright in his chair. But Jake wasn't in the room. He was carrying William out of the church, shoulder coffin-heavy numb, part of him torn away inside. Down the cemetery path and there he was, Charles beneath the distant tree. Jake almost stumbled with the blood running hot in his veins.

Watching William's coffin lowered down, reciting the poem Edith asked him to read, hands shaking the paper, ink bleeding... *I shall not see the shadows*... One eye on Charles... *shall not feel the rain*... The look on her face, slope of her shoulders...*dreaming through the twilight*... Strange wailing noise she made...*haply I may remember*. Wanting to climb down into the coffin and hold him again.

But children are only ever on loan to us.

Jake turned, eyeing the purple wing-back chair. Charles' hand on the chair arm, little finger flick-flicking. Jake scanned the shelves next to him. Books. Knick-knacks. Framed photographs. At first, he wasn't sure what he was looking at, but among the family portraits in a small, square photo frame, William's face was smiling back at him.

Jake cupped the frame in his hand. You could tell it was taken in winter and William was what, four or five years old? About to start school, maybe...

How vulnerable William looked among the other children in the playground. Having to deny the lad's emotions and fears because that was the necessary thing to do. No, you can't go back home. No. Go on, you'll be fine. It was brutal, having to let go when you've been at the centre of his world for the past five years and now there are other people populating his life. The whole sorry arse thing repeated when he hit puberty. Recalling his voice breaking somewhere around his thirteenth birthday. Edith found it funny, imitating him. Jake eyeing the lad, as if the man he was to become was about to crack through the ice. Losing the intimacy. No more bath times or drying him with a towel in front of the fire. No more cuddles at bedtime. And there was Jake trying to keep his innocence safe. Safe! William turning inwards into a man but he was still a little boy inside. Losing him at that point. Seventeen years old. Not seeing him fully transform into a man after all of that teenage angst and anguish. Such a waste. Flame red hair turned to rust.

Jake went over to Charles and crouched in front of him, his knees cracking. Something on Charles' ankle: a catheter tube, a bag of amber piss. Their eyes locked. There it was: the rhyme of it. How dare this half-man wear William's face!

Jake held up the photograph. Why do you have this?

Blinking now, Charles' mouth began to open and close like a hinge. Bony right-hand flapping about, quiver in his cheek, glisten of saliva on his chin.

M-m-m-m, Charles said, the answer emerging on his face.

What?

Charles' juddering arm moving towards the photo.

Mine, he said. Mine.

Jake dropped the photograph onto the carpet and reached towards Charles with both hands, finding the old man's windpipe, the rapid pulse. The strange groan and gurgling behind Charles' teeth as Jake squeezed with all his might—a song from the root of it all. The voice that had lived at the back of Jake's skull, tearing at his insides for forty-six years, it began in the Outwoods and nagged its way right up to this moment.

Mine, Jake said.

It didn't take long.

Jake got to his feet and stared down at the dead man. Charles' tongue hanging from his mouth like the labellum of some appalling orchid.

Jake turned and left the room, the nursing home. Left his old life behind.

Riding eighty miles east that night, following old drover's tracks over the uplands or sticking to the backroads and open fields, dipping down from Wensley to Howgrave, under the A1 to Carlton Minniot and Thirsk, hiding whenever he saw headlights on the horizon. Had he ever felt so alive? Then up the steep escarpment of Sutton Bank and through the open canopies of Helmsley Estate. He reached Dalby Forest in the middle of the night, 8,000 acres of broadleaf and pine on the southern slopes of the North York Moors, familiar to him from his years camping with William.

Present day

MIDDLE FORCE

Half braced against the tree, the front of him caked with snow, pain folds him up inside, each breath like pulling hot wire through his chest. He can't lift his left arm properly and so he slips a couple of rounds into the snow. But Lip isn't there anymore. It is only when he gets to his feet that he feels the red-hot poker in his hip. His trousers are shredded. He turns, aiming the barrel towards the drystone wall. Just the bones of the landscape, sky the colour of burnt milk. His eyes feel like ash. He wants to lie down and go to sleep. Arching his back with pain, he checks the wounds. Grim inventory. The bullet has just nicked his arm and passed through. The second in his right thigh near the groin, entry wound the size of an eye. Only difference between being alive and dead is me.

Howay.

He sets off, the blizzard moving over him, inside of him, everything so adrenalin vivid and unreal, the pain and snow becoming one.

Remembering William hiccupping breast milk down his neck. The way he'd always fill his nappy just as they were about to leave the house. Try to prize Jake's eyelids open with his sharp, tiny fingernails. Trudging through the pain, wading through the quag of memory, following the track carved through the snow by a farmer's quad delivering bales to the flock of Mashams gathered in a knot nearby on the fell. He wants to go over there and stick his face into the hay, smell the summer one last time. Squeaky crunch of his boots, snow scalloped by gusts of frost-filled wind, the mid-morning sun reaches across the landscape casting long blue shadows. In the distance, the limestone scars above Carperby. Almost home.

Snow devils whirl, gusts scalloping in scarfs of white, the ebb of fatigue and pain as he steps into a hagg, corvids chattering among the branches. He can barely keep his eyes open. Down through the trees towards Middle Force, snowflakes whipping this way and that, he reaches the cliff edge, peering down towards the cascades, bubbling and ecstatic in the bottom of the gorge.

Head upstream. Find the bridge. Home.

Peripherally he is conscious of a mutter behind him, a rustling in the leafless wood, and then the birds leap into the air, silhouettes against the cold tones of morning.

A figure running from the trees.

Jake scrambles for the rifle but drops it into a deep snowbank. He grabs the knife at his waist but in the same instant Lip is upon him. The force knocks Jake into the snow, head smacking off rock. The men tussle and growl. The dizzying ferocity of Lip's punches and kicks. Such carnal power and vengeance in the moment. The younger man is strong and coffin-nail thin. Lip clasps Jake's throat, squeezes. But it's William that Jake sees above him: same choirboy good looks, red-hair aflame. Jake stabs out with the hunting knife and it enters Lip's side, snagging on cartilage. Lip cries out in awful pain, blood and saliva swatting the snow. But now the knife is in Lip's hand and entering Jake's shoulder and arms, spraying coins of blood. Jake slams his fist into the side of Lip's skull and tries to kick the knife from his hand but Lip brings the blade down into his thigh with such force it splinters bone. Lip is on his feet, dragging Jake by the boots towards the cliff-edge. Jake reaches out, trying to hold onto something, but all he feels is snow. Look at pretty fowlers and flutterbies, Daddy! A hand in his, a tiny fish-white fist clinging onto his thumb, pair of orange eyes aflame amid the flakes. Peel the balala, Daddy! He's tumbling through the air, heartbeats counting off the seconds until he hits the water, their laughing faces distorted in the tumble of sky, water, sky. He's a tiny plastic figure in a snow globe, shaken roughly in Edith's hand.

Part TWO

FEBRUARY

Holding her hand under the shower until the water heats up, Sheila steps in and squeezes some shampoo into her palm and massages it into her scalp. Closing her eyes, she senses him again—the linger of him in the flat. He looked so thin and cold, coughing his guts up, the bob of his Adam's apple like a yo-yo in his throat. Removing his trapper hat, smoothing his hair, the way his hands shook—it made something come undone inside her.

And I cannot let you in.

She rinses the shampoo from her hair and applies some conditioner.

What if something has happened to him? How's that going to make her feel? Being so cold towards him.

She runs the conditioner through her hair and then shaves her armpits and legs.

The day she walked over to the caravan park on Jackson Bay but couldn't go in. He was in there, so close, no doubt scared and alone and she couldn't even bring herself to check on him, see he was all right.

She rinses and turns off the water and steps out. Wrapping a towel around her hair, she sits on the loo and brushes her teeth.

That shaky mobile phone footage of him on TV after rescuing the girl. For the few first days they thought he was just some random old guy or a homeless guy and even though you only see him from the back, walking away, Sheila knew it was him. She did some digging and found out where the girl lives—near to Falsgrave Park. Not entirely sure why. As if she was going to knock on the girl's front door and say, Hi, sorry to bother you, I'm a friend of the old guy that saved you. Yes, the one that murdered that other old man in the nursing home. Him!

She rubs a hole in the steam on the mirror and then uses a wet wipe to remove the remains of yesterday's mascara. She applies some eyeshadow, liner, and some shimmering light pink lipstick, and heads back into the bedroom. Sitting in front of the mirror, she forces a smile, examining her slightly crooked front teeth. Her damp hair is brown and scraggly, earth seeping through snow, the dirt he farmed, the ground he treads.

She puts a dollop of head defence cream into her palms and fingers it through the cotters in her hair. When she's done, she peers through the curtains—the moon is hanging enormous and bright above the castle.

She places a hand against her heart, feels the reassuring clatter.

On her days off she catches the train from Scarborough to York and then another up to Northallerton or Darlington where Bear picks her up from the station. He kisses her cheek with his bristle and engine and dog smell, but she can tell there's an enormous sigh fettered in him somewhere, because he'd rather they were alone together and doing owt but driving west through Swaledale and Wensleydale searching for Jake, wherever the hell he is. The soundtrack is usually Bear's Sabbath CDs but often the silences feel louder. Scouring the land outside the windscreen, she's sick of asking him to slow down. She knows he's right though—it's not as if Jake would've started walking back to the east coast again. He could be anywhere by now. Scotland. Wales. Cornwall. He was strong. Fitter than men half his age. Thoughts like these tumbling in her head and now she's chelping non-stop because she keeps thinking Bear knows summat.

She's always liked the way they interrupt each other and finish each other's sentences. It's like when they look at each other and they're on the verge of arguing and something lights them both from the inside and they can't help but smile.

The police found Jake's backpack in a field near Aysgarth, and now Lip Monroe was missing as well, which says something she doesn't even want to hear.

Bear lights another rollie. She lowers the window and shoves her nose into the rustling wind. Her thoughts turn to the jade plant in the window at home. The night Jake came around for tea and gave it to her.

Like putting a fingernail in soil and growing a whole new person.

They travel towards Hawes. Bear seems to think Jake would keep travelling west. Maybe he's staying with some old farmer-type he used to know. Over in the Lakes, maybe. They'll never catch him. He knows this land.

She looks at her hands. They're shaking.

Bear says, Spoke to Pete again last night.

Who?

The whipper-in. Fox hunting lot.

And?

Nowt.

Will you slow down, please?

Clouds gather the further west they drive. Sitting in silence, the musk of Bear's sweat in the car. He sits perfectly still like he's been carved from stone. Watching the blur of land outside, she thinks, again, about the night Jake turned up at her flat, how she almost told him: You've got nowt to go back to. Lip has destroyed it all. Burned it to the ground. What did you expect?

Dove Cottage with the overgrown garden and low-slung wall, the wooden shed with its slate roof reflecting the afternoon sun like a mirror—that's what she remembers. Picturing Jake chopping wood in the back garden, his trousers with the high waist and braces, shirtsleeves rolled up, knots of muscle in his forearms flexing.

Where are you?

The following morning, she sups coffee from her mug, watching Bear tinkering with the engine on his workbench. It is chilly in the garage but he is sweating in his overalls, dark patches under the arms and a V down his back. Wiping his hands on a rag, he looks her up and down. A few of the studs have popped loose at the front of his overalls and his chest hair is spiralled with sweat. This desire for him scares her. Where's it coming from? The menopause? The *moan*-opause. She needs hoeing, earth turning. She's the nail, Bear's the hammer.

He says, You sleep OK?

His oil-stained spare bedroom-cum-office.

Fine.

That bed OK?

The weird dips in the mattress. They bought it when they were first married and the troughs still hadn't filled out. Bedtime always used to be such a happy time. They never went to sleep on an argument. Not that they argued much. They liked eating and watching telly in bed. Two happy fatties stuffing their faces and laughing like numpties. He would always get up early and make her breakfast and a packed lunch. With Bear life was just so much more bearable.

What's wrong with me? she thinks. Why can't I just be normal? She had it so good with him and had thrown it all away. For what? She's a mystery to herself.

No idea, she said. Think I passed out. Didn't realise how long it would

152

take to get back last night. She hands him the mug of coffee. Finish it.

He scans her body again. Barely recognised you when I picked you up.

Could do with losing another few pounds.

Be nowt left.

Been through every single hole on my belt.

She hears herself, cringes.

She's shape-shifting. But where is this excess skin meant to go? Replacing fat for flaps of skin. Can people see it under her top? Maybe they think she's early-stage pregnant or it's a beer belly. So why does she feel such contempt towards her new, thinner body? Shouldn't she be pleased? Isn't it better for her heart and general health? She thinks she looks like a deflated balloon. And where are all of these chin hairs coming from? No, she thinks. I'm happy in my own skin, regardless of how much of it there is.

Bear cracks a half-smile. Time you due at the cop shop?

We're still unsure how much risk or danger Jake might be in, the officer says. We're taking the weather and his age into consideration, but according to interviews with yourself and other people that knew him—

I keep trying to convince myself he'll reappear.

That would be the best-case scenario. But we need to establish what Jake's state of mind was—

End of the summer. Last time I saw him, I mean.

The officer pauses. We both know that's not true.

Feeling see-through. Why haven't you found Lip Monroe?

He squints.

What'll happen if Jake doesn't turn up?

I'm afraid no death certificate, and therefore no grant, can be obtained.

Eh?

You'll have to speak to his solicitor about that side of things.

I don't care about any of that crap. Besides, it's got sod all to do with me. And why do you keep talking about Jake in the past tense?

A phone starts ringing in the other room.

And why keep mentioning a solicitor? Do you know summat I don't?

He opens his mouth, pauses. We can't declare a missing person deceased until after seven years.

Seven? That's ridiculous.

Later. Sheila and Bear head out into the glassy midwinter light in woollen hats, gloves and scarves, the dogs pulling at their leads and yapping. Moving through the empty streets of Nettlebed, they cross the beck into the park where they let the dogs off and they chase squirrels up the

154

trees. Bear puts his arm around her shoulder.

Reading her thoughts, he says, Jake. He'll be nodding off in front of an open fire somewhere. Glass of whiskey in his hand. Laughing about us all.

Are you sure, like, one-hundred per cent certain they didn't catch him?

Pete, the whipper-in. Says it was like Jake just disappeared that night. They picked up his tracks near Jervaulx. Then poof. Thin air.

Sheila falls quiet for a moment. Jake came from a dirt-poor family, she says. Did I tell you that? But they saw he was academically bright and he went to grammar school early. Put him up a year. He hated it. His family thought education was a way for him to escape the grind of working-class life, you know? Become summat better. But he rebelled and left school early and was taken on as a junior farmhand. Brief stint in the factory where he met Edith and then he was back to the land.

Why you telling me this?

Because I get it, she says. I get the pull.

I know you do, and I know you regret not doing the same. We always talked about getting a smallholding together. Remember?

She nods. Is no one saying owt about Lip? Lip's men, I mean?

No.

Night Jake turned up at mine. I should've gone to the police, right there and then. They would have protected him.

If you say so.

Maybe they would have been lenient. Him saving that lass from drowning.

None of this is your fault.

Could've pretended he was going senile or summat. I mean, what did Charles ever do to him? Jake's never mentioned him. Not once. Jake and Charles and Lip—it's totally pecking my swede. I mean, we all know they're stupid rich twats, but that doesn't mean... You sure you don't know owt?

The pause and stop of your heart just before the next beat, next pulse. The blood in your veins wavering, teetering. You wake up gasping, hands to your chest, clawing your breastbone as if trying to get inside and pump it manually. A sound filling your veins, vibrating around nothingness. Your mouth open in a silent scream.

MARCH

She finds the picture of Jake on her phone and looks at it for a long time. Lying here in the silent dark, wondering how soon she can have a drink. She tries her breathing exercises but nowt works. Why can't she get the idea of booze from her head? Gin. Bloody Mary. Cider with ice. A hoppy real ale. Cigarette. Yum.

There will be a period when her grief—because that's how it feels, like she has begun mourning Jake already—is replaced with a plain type of sadness. The type that is useful in that it dulls the edges and perhaps twenty minutes can pass during which the hurt and anger almost wanes. But it always returns with such venom.

She sits in the armchair and scans the room. She intended to decorate when she first moved in but never got around to it. She bought most of her furniture from the British Heart Foundation at the top of the street. Kept it minimal. She likes the fact the flat has an echo and she enjoys dusting the parquet floors, skating around the rooms, a damp cloth beneath each foot. But other than her framed photographs on the sideboard there is no unnecessary clutter, just an armchair and bed and a clothes rail, a scratched sideboard and a lavender scented candle on her bedside table. The small jade plant in her window, the cutting from the one Jake gave her last year. And the large gilt-framed mirror leaning against the bedroom wall, in front of which she stands every morning to examine her shrinking body.

Mirrors. Usually she doesn't mind what she sees reflected back. But some mirrors, like the ones in Dorothy Perkins, can eff right off.

She's had to buy new clothes and underwear and has dropped bra sizes, but parts of her body look deflated and she now has wiry black hairs sprouting from her chin as if her migration to Scarborough has triggered a move deeper into the menopause. Her periods are heavy, irregular, and her PMS is an effing nightmare. She often spends nights staring at the ceiling wide awake, listening to the neighbour clattering about upstairs. Emotionally, she is a car crash, an erratic pendulum, but she is determined not to become one of those women who has to tell every Tom, Dick and Harry about her hot flushes.

There it is again. The noisy sod upstairs. She can hear him cough, sneeze, crap, pee. A thump. A thwack. What sounds like singing or chanting.

She's had a couple of follow-up appointments at the cardiology department and is making good progress. She just needs to stick to her diet and exercise plan. But some mornings she awakes thinking about Jake and gets a tightness in her chest.

She takes her bag through to the bathroom and begins to position the driftwood and shells along the windowsill. She's running out of space.

So many dead moments since she moved to Scarborough, junctures bristling with regret and loneliness and boredom and worry. But she looks each moment in the eye and tells herself that pain is part of the process. This is what it costs to be free. And for the past couple of weeks, her large flat with its sea views and the surrounding narrow streets of the Old Town has begun to feel like home.

And then this.

She checks the time and does her make-up and heads into town. She buys a new top in the Next sale and then heads to her appointment at the hairdressers for a cut and blow dry and straighten.

The music in the waiting area is awful. Someone in the salon is fake-laughing. She checks her phone. Nowt. Checks the local news. Nowt. She eyes the stack of magazines. Don't do it. Those magazines are just put there just to make you feel worse about yourself, full of famous women with their slick hair tweaked to perfection, when your hair has its own peculiar waves and kinks and refuses to do what it's told and stay put, and any humidity or drizzle or rain (and of course you always leave the house without a brolly) and it goes frizzy and boings up into a strange coif. Ugh.

But how can you do such a thing? What kind of woman buys herself a new top and goes to the hairdressers when their friend is on the run? What kind of woman does that?

This kind.

But maybe it's a form of what's it called? Masochism. Having a ruddy mirror stuck in front of your face and putting up with the inane tittle-tattle and the end result is always so effing disappointing. The fact you're supposed to know the names of styles and look after your hair and go regularly. The way they ask what you would like today but then they always do whatever they frigging want. Cut way too much off or make you look like the women on the Boots perfume counter.

But she does like getting her head massaged and the free drinks and sometimes the free products. But not the music today. Rarely the music. Sometimes you're in here for a long effing time and you expect good tunes to get you through.

She loves being blonde. How the shape of her hair falls around her face. She even loves its kink, sometimes. How changing its colour can do weird things like make her eyes look bluer. Make her look more alert and awake. How cutting it can make her feel like she's got a brand-new face. But hair means more to her than she is likely to admit. As a woman, it is something you are defined by throughout your life (alongside all the other bollocks). Blonde bombshell. Fiery redhead. Cute pigtails. Luscious curls. Eff that.

Two hours later and her hair is done with the usual cabin-crew effect and Sheila pays and pretends it's the BEST haircut she's EVER had. Usually she would go straight home to wash it, but sod it—she needs a drink.

The Merchant. She's on good terms with the staff and the regulars, mostly a few of the regular fishermen that come in on their tour of the harbour pubs. The manager, Dai, is a stocky half-asleep kind of guy who looks like he has been carved from a tree trunk. White polo shirts with the collar turned up or a stained Foo Fighters T-shirt. An accent that shifts between West Country and valley Welsh. He is usually sat at the bar reading a Harlan Coben novel or cleaning his wire-framed spectacles. A widower, he likes to flirt with Sheila and Sheila likes to flirt back.

He keeps buying her drinks and she keeps knocking them back and puffing on his Strawberry Muffin Man e-cigarette. She's telling him about her heart attack and losing so much weight and the self-loathing because she isn't taking care of herself lately. How she needs to stick to the diet and rehab plan or before you know it she'll be a heifer again and having another cardiac event.

He says a lot of nice things and she almost believes him.

Then she mentions Jake's disappearance and she flushes angrily and tells him the truth.

Yes, I know him. At least I thought I did.

And then they are back at his pokey flat, sitting on his settee, and Dai is holding her in his big hairy arms when he kisses her cheek and does it again and she moves her mouth onto his and he kisses her so hard she thinks her lips might bruise.

The banging of bodies in the dark. The pong of his e-cigarette waking her in the middle of the night. Feeling him on top of her for the second time and she nearly suffocates—a strange feeling of déjà vu creeping over her.

The next morning, she awakes to find a Welsh dragon tattoo in her face. Beneath his gingery pelt: red scratch marks. She checks her hands. One of her nails is broken. Slut! She is so thirsty, the bed so lumpy. The sour smell of his coarse bedsheets. She checks her watch and rubs at the soreness between her breasts and then creeps out of bed and freezes as he turns over and grunts. She can't find her knickers. She dresses and sneaks out into the shame of the morning light.

A chill easterly brings gales and the frosty snap of the Urals and it stirs in her a longing for the summers when she was a teenager and life was so much simpler. Hers was a tiny room with a single bed against one wallpaper-picked wall, looking out over an expanse of field and fell, the sound of Mam clattering about in the kitchen downstairs, the house smelling of apple pie. She would sit by her window for hours watching the clouds scroll by, wishing she was far away from here. On a frigate with Dad in the South China Sea. That feeling, like she was missing out on something. Life was happening elsewhere. Her bedroom window looking out over the Pick Your Own fruit and vegetable farm. She loved collecting her punnet and crouching amid the rows beneath a punishing sun—one for the punnet, one for the gob, fingers and lips stained pink, belly full and aching.

She hit puberty and became chubby and strong. Mam got her a job on the farm when she turned fourteen, cash-in-hand, weekends and holidays. Sheila grafted and saved and no matter how wasted on cider she was the night before, she was never late for work, never missed a day. She gave the farm lads as good as she got.

Last night's snowfall melts in the crisp morning light, igniting icicles dripping onto the salty street outside her living room window. The snow has composed rooflines that are soft, hemming in the narrow streets of the Old Town. She pulls the curtains closed and admires the wine juice light seeping through the purple fabric. She glances around the room remembering Jake being here. Tincture of his stress and desperation in the air. The way he moved around the room as if stepping into surf—the consequences of his actions sweeping him out to sea.

She pulls on her coat, grabs her handbag and crunches down the salted lanes through an eddy of snowflakes. Stepping into the warm café, she bids the waitress a good morning and takes her usual table beside the window. The wind is getting up outside, making the strings of lights clatter against the panes. The gentle warm bustle of a little café with cut flowers in glass beakers on the tables and flowery tablecloths. She removes her heart pills and arranges them on the table and half-smiles at them like old friends. Unzips her parka, warms her fingers against her cheeks. The waitress comes and takes her usual order: 'fare-thee-well Prison Eggs'—scrambled eggs (without butter or milk), jalapenos, borlotti beans and spring onion—and a cup of green tea, black, no sugar. Joy! She rubs a hole through the condensation on the window and the porthole reveals waves crashing against Vincent's pier. Then she watches the waitress prepare the café for the day, working at speed, wiping the tables and menus and chairs, folding napkins and rolling silverware. She's a good little grafter. More customers arrive. Two fat old ladies—regulars. The waitress greets and seats them and takes their order, even though they have the same fry-up and pot of tea every day. Pretty soon more customers trickle in.

The waitress brings Sheila's order over and, as she begins to tuck in, Jake crashes her thoughts again. His disappearance has tainted her life. Her days feel fake.

Recently she has started to notice the chavs who usually congregate by the Job Centre steps at night, all swagger and gob. Were there always this many? And the sounds of the town are different. It's either the music from their mobile phones or the late-night shouting from folk leaving the pub or the ceaseless wind coming in off South Bay. No one meets your eye. No one says hello any more.

Jake's disappearance has left her feeling unanchored. The almost fifty-one-year-old Sheila doesn't know who she is any more. She is a stranger to herself, living in a stranger's flat. Wrong flat, wrong town. And there is no way she can ever get home again. To find it is all a dream. To find Jake sitting in his usual chair in the Ox.

Another round, Jake? You bastard.

Late afternoon, she is in her tiny kitchenette waiting for the kettle to boil when she hears a noise coming from the stairwell. She rushes along the corridor and puts her eye to the peephole. It's the neighbour from upstairs—bearded, pony-tailed, skinny black trousers and leather jacket. He ascends the stairs slowly, yawning dramatically. Above her, the thump of his front door closing, clomp of footsteps along the hallway. She pictures him at his bay window gazing out at the sea.

Later. She has just got into bed when the banging starts. It is almost midnight and she is up at five. She switches off her lamp and spreads starfish in the dark. The sound increases, her heart racing like a hamster in its wheel. She gets out of bed and heads into the kitchen, gets the mop, climbs onto a chair and bangs the handle against the ceiling a few times. Between her ragged breaths, silence.

Wanker! she shouts.

The following evening. Bear is picking her up in half an hour and she is just stepping out of the shower when the banging starts again. She pulls on her dressing gown and takes the stairs up to her neighbour's flat and thumps on his door.

The sound stops. She thumps again.

A Viking answers the door. Breathing heavily, face flushed, he's wearing a brown woollen tunic fastened with a large belt from which hangs a knife and there's an iron helmet on his head and in his right hand, a large ornate sword—he raises it into the air and cries, An axe-age, a sword-age, shields will be cloven!

Have you any idea how frigging loud you are?

He cradles the sword against his chest. I didn't—

Well keep it down, you plank. I work shifts.

She turns and heads back down the stairs.

Sorry, he shouts down after her.

Bear drives them over the snow-covered moors. The roads are quiet and the heated seat makes her feel a tad sleepy. She doesn't want to be here but she has to do something to break her out this thing she has been ambushed by—something like mourning and shock and anger. A flurry of snow comes slantwise as they reach the high limestone summit near Malham Tarn, the sides of the road deep with ploughed snow. He drops the car down into second, hunched over the wheel, squinting between the wipers.

She says, Do you remember us visiting Kilnsey Park?

The orchid place?

They visited the park's Wild About Orchids festival a few years back, and laying her eyes on the Lady's Slipper orchid for the first time, just being in its presence, years after the species had been declared extinct— it was one of the most intense moments of her life.

This is stupid, she says.

He glances at her.

They drop down towards Arncliffe, the white-out broken occasionally by longhouse laithes and drystone walls and telegraph poles. Passing over the cattle grid, the snow pauses and the settlement reveals itself in the dale bottom, a huddle of tan sandstone and limewash. And as stupid and pointless as it might be—driving through this snowy wilderness looking for Jake—she can't deny it: it feels so nice being in the car with Bear. Just being together, side by side, driving kind of aimlessly across the Dales.

Later. Sitting at the kitchen table opposite him, the dogs steaming and stinking in front of the fire, she realises Bear looks different. She knows all of his expressions, as if they are masks he can pull on at will. But this one is new.

She excuses herself and goes to the toilet and sits holding her head in her hands. Sweating, she's worried she is going to have another cardiac.

Her phone buzzes. It's Dai.

She can still feel him under her skin. And with all of these re-emergent feelings for Bear running amok inside her—

Hello, she says to herself. You massive dozy twat.

She flushes the loo, washes her hands and heads back into the kitchen.

You OK? he says. You look queer.

I'm fine.

She notices a mark on the bridge of his nose. He has a habit of scratching himself in his sleep. She taps her nose.

He says, It's these strips I'm wearing. Stops me snoring.

They working?

Feel better in the morning. Must be doing summat.

(Let's pretend nowt's wrong.)

She says, And what about your left nut?

Still hurts. Nowt I can't live with.

You need to empty your sack more often.

Is that an offer?

She raises a brow.

I swear, he says, the only events in my life nowadays are medical.

So, you been keeping someone awake at night with your snoring?

He frowns.

She says, You're not seeing anyone?

Nope.

And?

And what?

Dai comes into the bar carrying a box of crisps and when he sees Sheila a thrill lights his face. She doesn't know what she's doing here. He places the box on the floor and gives her a hearty hug.

Thought you'd left town, he says, and plants a peck on her cheek.

She opens her mouth.

He says, What?

She eyes the dregs in the bottom of her glass.

He gestures to the barman and then pulls up a stool next to her.

She returned to Scarborough last week with something resembling relief. Never—not even during the early years when they were married—had she talked to Bear so much. Really opened up to him. As if Jake's disappearance has exposed something new inside of her. She adores being around Bear again. Allowing him, for once, to see the other side to her, a softer side she closed down years ago.

So what the hell was she doing here?

Dai says, Thought I'd done something to upset you, and she recalls the last time she saw him, the walk of shame through the early morning sea-fret, wanting to get home and wash him from her body, wash the bruises from her skin, like the blooms of tiny flowers.

She makes her excuses and leaves.

The evenings turn milder over the next few days, the rise in temperature bringing days of dense sea-fret and mizzle, loosening the remaining snow on the uplands, and she notices not only the way it flattens the views but how it blurs the land itself, how it mutes the daily sounds, bringing everything nearer and yet out of focus. Then a northerly blasts down from the Arctic, blanketing the uplands white. Winter clinging on.

Jake, out there in all of this. Alone. Lost to himself.

APRIL

The mother and son pass a dead badger on the grass verge and she holds her nose and says, They're coming out of hibernation. The big sleep. Staggering around like they're drunk and get splattered. Breaks my heart.

They cross the bridge and follow the beck, the scratch of birdsong all around. She points out how the hedgerows are already in flower, buds on the hawthorn with their smell like unwashed armpits and the twigs on the birch trees filling with sap. They find a way-sign and cross a stile and pass through a farm's in-bye land and soon they reach the woodland surrounding the falls. Amid the trees, she points out new shoots of holly and rowan.

The bluebells have gone already, she says with sadness.

The son peers up. A couple of crows are doing some raucous mating in the treetop.

They hear the thunge and hiss of the lower falls before they can see them. Passing through a couple of kissing gates, they scramble down a grassy bank and over some boulders and find a perch to sit on. They open their packed lunches and a flask to share, watching the water hurling itself down the staircases of rock, chatting as a knot of tiny birds flicker through the reeds beside them.

She smiles at him, tips the coffee dregs out, passes the cup back. Thanks.

Gingerly they step closer to the water, the churn and bubble, the suck and clatter. The son stops talking, stares at his mother. She is examining something. She points. There are two jackdaws at the foot of the waterfall, observing them with beady obsidian eyes before flying away. Then another jackdaw appears from behind the falls, and another. Apart from the birds' grey hoodies, their bodies are so black, so dark, as if they are made of night, of deepest space, and their thin chatter sounds more like laughter, a clucking of tongues. They alight with a scalding *aaar, aaar, aaar*.

Mother and son share a look and move closer.

Around the curtain of water, the mother pushes her face into the dank, dark womb.

It's a cave, she says.

Then she sees it. The drafty onrush of the foss mixing with her moans.

No, she says. No.

What?

The son steps past her, ducking low into the cave. Images vanish and reappear, thin and trembling like phantoms. He can't stop looking. On the cave floor, a corpse beyond dead, beyond yeasting, ragged mask of skin hanging loose on the skull, pink-white eyeholes scoured clean as stone, gashes beneath the cheekbones, purple tongue-root visible where bird's beaks made ingress. Stabbing. Routing.

No, the mother says again.

The storm brings the warm day to an epileptic close, continuing to rattle throughout the night. Sheila keeps re-running the police officer's words in her head: Evidence at the scene strongly suggests—

What evidence? What details?

It's Jake, he said bluntly. I'm sorry, Sheila.

Imagining his final moments curled up in the cold and dark cave. Eyes not seeing, ears not listening, heart lamenting no more.

So many questions.

She climbs from the spare bed, crumps into the kitchen and opens the back door. Stench of sodden earth, petrichor. On the doorstep in her knickers and T-shirt, she watches the rain coming down in an endless sheet, percussive drops bickering the shed roof, the sound of so many sighs. She stretches out her hand to feel it on her skin. Then she moves into the garden in her bare feet. Drenched already, she pulls her T-shirt up over her head and steps out of her knickers. Naked among the tall grass, she extends her arms, curling mud between her toes, tilting her head back and opening her mouth, the rain like pinpricks. *And I cannot let you in*. She is thinking about the moment Jake took her in his arms and sang to her, the way they moved together, the hot flutter and sway, spinning on an axis through the cold dark space of her soul, and she is experiencing something similar now, becoming bodiless at the moment of impact—embracing the rain, becoming more than herself.

MAY

She receives a phone call from a solicitor in Nettlebed asking her to visit his office.

Sitting behind his large wooden desk, he's a nervy man, the sort who speaks with his hands. He has a small circular tuft of hair in the centre of his bald head, a little island of denial.

I can't imagine what a difficult time this must be for you. Can I get you a drink?

I'm fine.

Behind him, a bookcase runs the full length of the wall. A half-dead plant sits in the corner and the dusty blinds look like they have never been opened. Beside his laptop, aligned in symmetry: phone, notepad, pen, watch. He has that dusty solicitor essence: lever arch files. Post-It notes. Chewed up pen lids.

He slides a piece of paper towards her. As Jake named both you and myself as executors of his will—

Eh?

It is our responsibility to give effect to his funeral wishes.

Funeral wishes?

If you could turn to page two.

She glances down at the will, spreading her fingers on top of it.

It's all happening so fast, she says. None of this makes sense.

I'm sympathetic to your situation. However, we have to make sure Jake's estate is administered correctly. That his wishes are followed. I can start the process today by applying for the Grant of Representation.

She stares at him.

Once the coroner has issued the Certificate of the Fact of Death and authorised the release of Jake's body—

He is saying something about a direct cremation and that Jake didn't want a funeral, that the paperwork will have to go back and forth between the funeral director and crematorium.

However, let me reiterate, you are the sole beneficiary of this agreement. I can make decisions in your best interests but other than my fee I have no vested interest in the estate. Then he says it again: Cremation Six Form.

If his face were a noise it would be the sound of crashing cymbals.

I'll pay the fee when the time comes but that doesn't mean we can't get the ball rolling. And I'll have to send a copy of the death certificate to organisations such as banks and building societies and find out if Jake owed money to creditors. And I'm sorry to be so blunt, but if the inquest determines Jake took his own life then his life insurance will be invalidated.

She scoffs. Think we both know what happened.

He pauses. In the will, Jake bequeathed to you his property, Dove Cottage.

Sheila snorts a laugh. Brilliant. And what the hell am I meant to do with a burned-down house? Eh? There's nowt left. And the council haven't even cleared it yet. Useless gets. Suppose I'm going to have cough up for it?

He says, I'll deal with the insurance side of things. Then he slides a piece of paper over to her. Jake also bequeathed to you the money in his savings account.

She looks at the figure, looks at the solicitor. He raises his hands above the table, like the edges of a thought bubble—but there's nowt inside. No words. No sentiments.

He says, And there's the land. Freehold. Just over 10,000 square feet. That's about a quarter of an acre.

I know what a bloody acre is.

Sorry.

She eyes the large sum again. Can I ask you summat?

A-huh.

I take it Jake came to see you not long before—you know?

He nods.

Did you have any inkling? That he had owt planned, I mean? Owt that made you think…?

I've thought about it a lot. But no. Nowt.

A moment passes. They adjust their positions.

She says, He's in a fridge.

Sorry?

They've taken bits away and what's left is in a fridge? Naked on a table. Scalpels. Something at the nape of his neck, propping up his skull.

He clears his throat.

Sorry, she says, and rubs her eyes, smudging her mascara.

She signs the paperwork and leaves the office feeling like a character in a novel, because Jake has created a whole new narrative for her, an entirely new storyline, forcing an intersection in her life with something she doesn't yet fully understand.

The following morning on Potters Row, twenty-four identical bungalows facing each other with their brightly painted doors. The sky is beginning

173

to bleach the eastern horizon, illuminating the roof lines, and all is quiet until a blackbird, perched on a TV aerial, puffs up his chest and begins a duet with another, more distant bird. In the end bungalow, in the tiny box room, Sheila stirs. Her back hurts. Her nightshirt is claggy with sweat. She nods back off.

dream

She is in bed watching a film on her laptop, the blue of the screen illuminating her face. Someone enters the bedroom: it's her, Sheila, but a younger version. Sheila when she was in her twenties. Two Sheilas in the room divided by thirty years. Young Sheila mouths *Thank you* and pulls back the duvet and climbs in. The two of them falling asleep in each other's arms—

Sheila?

A hand on her shoulder.

Sheila?

It's Jake, his ghost leaning into her dreams. He's sitting in the chair beside the bed, long ear hairs lit in the sunlight streaming through the curtains. The glitter to his eyes when he grins, showing so great against his weathered skin—such detail.

She awakes.

Sound of the bin men in the street outside. Radio in the kitchen.

Jake. Dead.

The room is cluttered and chintzy and too warm for comfort. Mam looks flummoxed, a certain hardness in her gaze. She didn't take the news of the will very well last night. Not thinking about Sheila, of course. Just thinking about what folk will say. Though Sheila didn't mention the money. She isn't going to tell anyone.

Sheila tends to chelp when Mam is in one of her peppery moods. She says, I told Karen. I says to her, I says, get your name on the council

174

waiting list. Get you and the bairn a nice flat. Don't rely on fatso Mike. I says, you can't rely on men full stop. And I told Bear he has to help out more with her and the bairn.

Mam nods, hums, her eyes narrowing with that particular cat-like smugness she keeps in reserve for moments like this. Recently there has been something numb and distant inside her Sheila can't reach—some dark kernel.

Sheila sighs and squints at the framed photograph of her dad on the mantelpiece. Dad in his blue No. 1 dress about to meet the Duke of Edinburgh. Double-breasted reefer jacket, peaked cap, medals. Handsome, dapper. The curl of his lip in the image—on the edge of laughter.

They married way too young and Mam was always quick to tell you this. They were at a party when he appeared, tall and shiny and nervous in his able seaman uniform. She knew he was The One and they danced and kissed that night and within a year they were married and posted abroad. She quickly realised she hated the navy life but she had a bun in the oven so she could lump it. Pictures of her back then show a pretty young woman who looks a little tired, sad.

It was tough having a dad in the Navy. His duty always came first. Deployments lasted between six to nine months with the opportunity to fly home for three or four days halfway through. The longest stretch was while he was on an Arctic survey ship—he was away two whole years. It was like the family was constantly on the verge of collapse due of this invisible third party and he missed all the important stuff like birthdays and Christmases. His homecomings were always such a mixed bag because although it was so good to see him they knew he'd be leaving soon. Mam had to be a rock.

Sheila turns to Mam. I says to Bear, I says, she can stay at yours a couple of nights a week as well and no excuses about the ruddy dogs. Keep them in the shed if you're that bothered. He treats them like they're bairns.

Mam squints at her, pouts.

Do you want to say summat, Mam?

Me? No, love.

Sheila grips the chair's arms, knuckles turning white.

I don't appreciate your tone, Sheila says.

Beg your pardon?

You heard, you old goat. If you've summat to say, just say it.

They are silent for a few seconds until Mam reaches for the remote and the din of the TV fills the room. Ignoring each other in unnameable silence.

The next morning, Sheila joins the queue at the café in the indoor market. Listening to the customers behind her: an elderly couple having a restrained argument and a guy with a chinstrap beard jabbering into his mobile phone. She tries not to make eye contact or stand too close to anyone because she is worried they can smell it on her: the sense of Jake and what he's done. Occasionally someone will stare at her, through her, perhaps sensing something not quite right, at a loss.

Yes, love?

Tuna sandwich, please.

White, brown or granary?

Granary.

The old couple, she realises, are arguing about her.

Jake. Dead.

Later, strolling around the estate, she stops outside the house where her best friend at school—Jude—used to live. She eyes the top left window, grins. At first, they avoided each other because Jude was an unknown quantity. She'd been through the care system and had spent time in a reception unit, place of screams and kids with hard eyes. Then she was fostered by a family in Nettlebed and met Sheila. Though in some ways high school was worse than the reception unit. The way teenage girls look at each other, always comparing. Initially, Sheila and Jude bonded over bitching about everybody else, especially the whiny first years. They mimicked and teased them, but quickly they came to turn on each other in the way close friends do, their friendship an endless stream of dark insults that became more sinister the closer they got. At times, they even shocked themselves. I can't believe you just said that! Those hot summer days on Jude's bed, kissing and touching each other. No, you be the boy. Then she was adopted and after two long awkward letters she stopped writing. Sheila knew why: she was happy with her new family. She didn't want to rub it in.

A week later Sheila is back in Scarborough. She has a couple of glasses of wine and watches TV and then heads to bed early. Staring at the ceiling, listening to the Viking knobhead clattering about upstairs. The rain starts. A forceful rain. A hish and thrum against her sash windowpanes. She sighs and rolls onto her side and thinks about sleeping in Bear's spare bed last week. How she'd wanted him to come down in the night and get in beside her. So much pent up want in that week of anger and upset. Again, she looks at the picture of Jake on her phone, thinking about his large callused hand on her waist. Then she thinks about Bear's hands: carburettors, leather, patchouli oil, diesel and dog's licks. The many engine scars he's superglued together.

She buries her face in her pillow and screams.

That Friday night she is in the corridor of the Merchant, wobbly from cider and desperate for the loo but someone is being sick inside, and out of nowhere she remembers a house party when she was what, eight or nine? Watching Mam and Dad sitting on the settee together, Mam sitting in Dad's lap, burying her face in his neck. Smiling widely, they stroked each other's fingers like they were relaying secret messages. Then Dad squeezed Mam tightly and they held each other's gaze in some kind of mind-read. But then something happened. Mam's visual silence and acid smile. A flick of the head and the way she let her hair cover her eyes, hiding her thoughts. Then Mam stood up and pointed at Dad but Sheila couldn't make out what they were saying. Dad left for sea the next day.

She makes herself spag bol with Quorn mince and microwaved rice and opens a bottle of Chilean red. She lays the table, lights a candle and puts some music on the dock.

INXS doing 'Need You Tonight'.

Sitting at the table, lifting the first forkful of spagbol to her mouth, she pauses. She sees herself as if she's standing on the other side of the room: a middle-aged woman eating on her own and necking a bottle of vino to herself. Was this how it starts? Before long she'll be like Mam, looking forward to her fish supper from the chippy and tonight's episode of *Corrie*, farting in her nightgown.

The song ends.

In the silence, she can hear the Viking clomp above.

Jake. Dead.

She climbs the stairs and knocks on his door. He's dressed normally this time—hair down, cardigan and jeans and a pair of thick black-rimmed spectacles.

Just wondering if you've eaten?

With an index finger he pushes his spectacles up the bridge of his nose.

I've made too much, she says. Be a shame to let it go to waste.

He continues staring at her.

The offer's there. Neighbours talk to each other where I come from.

What is it?

Quorn spag bol.

Any chillies in it?

No.

I'll bring my own.

He raises his wine glass and says, We give thy humble thanks for this thy special bounty. They chink glasses. Does he realise he is still wearing his Shawn the Sheep slippers? Sheila has started to warm towards this odd man and she savours the fact he won't raise the spectre of Jake. They finish the food and she opens another bottle of red. He compliments her musical taste. He has what she calls a 'heart laugh' and he is quick-witted and very chatty. In the space of an hour she discovers his name is Lucas (never Luke), he is 36 years old and in love with 'a big hairy mountain man' but the love isn't reciprocated.

In a burst, he adds, I like real fires, music, parties, takeaways, beards, books, laughing, clichés, cities, lakes, vodka, sarcasm and purple. He inhales deeply. And Vikings.

What is it with them?

Yorkshire's Scandinavian heritage. The theatre of it all. Dressing up. Camaraderie. It's just a shed-load of fun. The woodland battlefields are my fave. I just love forest bathing. The Japanese call it *shinrin yoku*. You can find happiness in the simplest of things—swimming in becks, watching clouds, climbing trees...

For a few minutes, she forgets about Jake.

She says, Re-enactments. They always remind me of Monty Python.

There is that.

So, what's your Viking name?

I'm Ottar, son of Bjorn the Eastman. From the Laxdaela Saga. I wanted to be Thorgils Skarthi who ruled over Scarborough, but he was taken.

Weirdo.

What about you? I take it you're not married? Not seen any fellas around.

And there we have it.

What?

It's called a private life for a reason.

Sorry.

Don't be. It's me. I'm not very well what's-the-word? Socialised.

You're right though. Folk want to know your ins and outs. *Literally*.

We're separated. Still good friends. But I'm happy on my own, thanks.

Liar.

It's that obvious?

What's your type?

Same as you by the sounds of it. I want a man that will give the greatest hugs and smile at me when I walk in a room.

Lucas says, Kismet.

What?

It's your destiny. I can feel it.

She tops up his wine glass. His face is flushed, eyes vibrant.

I'll need to go after this, he says. Got to give a presentation at work in the morning and I'm proper bricking it.

You'll be fine.

Mountain Man will be there.

Just imagine him naked.

It's all I ever do. So, what about the future?

What about it?

If you could do owt?

I want to learn to surf and scuba dive.

Really?

As if. I don't know. Travel more.

You got any tattoos?

I hate needles.

Lucas extends an arm. In the crook of his elbow are the words: *we're made from the mistakes we make*. On his wrist: four stars.

The constellation of Gemini, he says. You have Scorpio or Sagittarius traits. He downs his wine and gets to his feet. Let's go for a drink some time. It'll be fun.

I'd like that, she says.

After work the following day, she turns the corner of her street to find Dai waiting on her doorstep.

I called, he says.

My phone's off.

Right.

I have the work one on, just not my personal one.

Can I have your work number?

No.

She has a sudden flash-back: Dai is kissing her belly button. No, not kissing it—he's licking it, sticking his tongue *right in there*. Ugh. Remembering this, she feels violated. That scar belongs to Karen!

Look, she says. I really need to crash.

I wanted to talk to you about Friday. Going for a meal. You said—

I was drunk.

But—

Stop mithering me, man.

He reaches into his jacket pocket and hands her a piece of material. Thought you might like these back?

It's her knickers.

She says, You're a charmer, aren't you? She turns the key in the lock, steps into the house and slams the door behind her.

Later. Sitting by the window in the café, the expansive view of the sea reveals itself. A column of sunlight falls aslant through a break in the quilt-like cloud and the sea moves through a shifting pattern of colours. Her mobile rings. It's the solicitor.

He says, I'll sort out the necessary paperwork and fees and collection for the crematorium and let you know when he's ready to pick up. Or I can arrange a courier?

What? Stick Jake in the post? No. I'll come get him. I'm back in Nettlebed on Friday.

She hangs up. She places her finger against her wrist, rocking slightly to the tempo of her pulse. Her bra is itching like crazy. When she looks down her top she finds it is inside out.

As she leaves the café, she texts Dai.

Please remove my number from your phone.

JUNE

Bear looks solid, serene. Seeing him is a shot in the arm. Though she spent most of the afternoon freaking out because she didn't know what to wear. Fifty-one-years-old today, and nowt, for some reason, seems to fit. The Italian in Leyburn is all woody décor and simple chairs. An open-plan kitchen, flirty waiters and the heady scent of oregano. She can't remember the last time they went for a meal. Yonks.

She gave him strict instructions: they weren't to talk about Jake.

Do not mention the J-word!

Sheila orders Spaghetti Napoli, and Bear, Steak Diane. They eat in silence. She keeps thinking about what Lucas said: that she should tell Bear how she feels. She drains her prosecco, enjoying the fizz in her mouth. She lifts the empty glass, catches a waiter's eye. She knows she should order a bottle. Bear restarts the earlier conversation about Karen.

He says, I feel a bit out of my depth if I'm honest.

Don't talk daft. You're a great dad.

(And I love you, she says in her heart.)

Their eyes lock in the flicker of candlelight. The waiter refreshes Sheila's glass. She picks up her cutlery and devours the last of the spaghetti, splashing her blouse a little but she doesn't care. She drains half of the prosecco in one.

So, what you're saying is you want me to talk to her?

A-huh.

Fat lot of good that'll do.

Try.

Like it'll make any sodding difference?

There's summat else.

What?

Mike hasn't been paying the rent.

Idiot.

There's been complaints about the noise. Parties. The council gave him ample warning. The neighbour has MS and ended up in hospital with the stress. So, they're booting them out.

You're just telling me this now?

I've only just found out. You know what she's like. She's like you: good at pretending nowt's up.

Happy birthday, Sheila mutters.

Mike reckons he's got it under control. Somewhere for them to stay.

Muppet.

She peers around at the other diners. The way Bear can deliver all of this so calmly and then start chewing away on his steak. She scratches at something on her chin. A hair. A thick, bastard hair.

I'm off to the loo, she says, and grabs her handbag.

She sits in a cubicle with her compact and plucks the offending article. She sighs the sigh of the beaten. Her daughter, soon to be homeless. Not like that would ever happen. But still. She takes out her phone and starts to compose a text to Karen but she knows it'll only make things worse.

She feels like such a bad mother. Worse than that, she feels useless in the face of it all. Jake. Karen. Mam. Bear. Clem. Charles and Lip Monroe. Nettlebed. What folk must think. The nagging fret.

But she was more than that.

Lately, she has been thinking about her grandson's future. The sort of person he'll turn out to be. Will he be nice? Will he have kids or not want kids? Will he be straight or gay or bi? Will he be a wage-slave or a dole scrounger? Will he be an internet troll? Will he run marathons? Will he travel or become so obese he rarely leaves the house? Will he function? Will he care? Or will he be a selfish prick like his dad?

And Karen?

Sheila hates the fact that

—she's a liar.

—everything is always someone else's fault.

—she's a work-shy slob who has all the ailments under the sun.

—she hides behind Clem and probably won't give him opportunities to flourish in life.

—she overshares her private life all over social media.

—she never sends Mam a birthday or Christmas or thank-you card for all that she does.

—she made giving birth look so easy. She was almost completely effing silent. (Sheila was in labour with Karen for fifty-eight hours and the blood and contractions were infinite.)

—she's on her mobile phone constantly, interrupting conversations when she receives a message, talking way too loud, every sentence ending with 'like' or 'youknowhatimean?'

Attention-seeking Karen. Hair-sniffing Karen.

But Sheila knows everyone has a maze inside them and Karen has her own to work through, until you discover the dark secret at the centre. That's where your own personal monster lives. Most people spend their lives trying to work their way out of their maze.

Tomorrow, she tells herself, I'll go see her. Talk to her. Sort this mess out once and for all.

She flushes the loo and washes her hands, looking at herself in the mirror.

Sheila knows her monster well—it is staring right back at her.

She returns to Scarborough the following evening. Karen refused to see her. She wouldn't even answer the door. And as soon as Sheila steps off the train she feels so lonesome—she can't recall a time she has missed Bear and Karen and Mam so much. She wanders home through the dark rainy streets. Her flat feels cavernous. She knocks on Lucas's door and then tries to phone him and he texts back to say he is at some re-enactment event in York. It only sinks her mood further. She heads straight to bed.

The following day is bright and blowy as she walks along South Bay, but the view through her sunglasses does nowt for her. She makes her way up South Cliff as the sky darkens. She pulls up her hood and finds shelter beneath a tree near a pub in Ramshill. Then it starts to sile it down. She dashes into the pub where the doughy-faced punters ogle her. She orders a drink and takes a seat at the far end and hangs her coat to dry on the back of a chair. Notices a UKIP poster in the window. She picks up the newspaper and reads while sipping her cider. To look at her you would think she was totally absorbed in the paper but her mind is meandering.

Over the next few days she tries to spend as little time on her own as possible. When she isn't at work she explores the shops and museums and library and the seafront arcades and pops into pubs she's never been into before, giving Dai and the Merchant a wide berth. One fine evening she walks for miles along the Cleveland Way, almost to Knipe Point. Standing on the cliff edge, thinking: What the hell am I still doing here?

When she gets to work the following evening, her boss calls her into his office.

Folk have been singing your praises, he says. Don't look so surprised. A vacancy has opened up for a deputy branch manager at Normanby House.

Are you trying to get rid of me?

He laughs. Look, you've more nouse than the other staff put together. You interested?

She starts to cry. A wracking, completely over-the-top bawling. A tissue is being held in front of her face and she takes it and drenches it with her misery and self-loathing and then drops it on the floor. They both stare at it.

Morning. She returns to the flat to the sound of Lucas's footfalls. She stomps upstairs and knocks on his door.

She says, What you up to today?

Nowt.

Fancy a walk to Filey? Get some scran in a pub afterwards? My shout.

The pub is quiet. Sheila places her hands around her pint glass and stares at it for what feels like a long time.

Lucas says, You OK?

A baby starts grizzling and wailing on the other side of the room. Sheila sups the foam of her pint and wipes her lips with the back of her hand.

I've been having crazy dreams, she says.

He scrutinises her. What kind of dreams?

I dream that my heart stops. But in the dream I wake up to find I'm still alive. But something isn't quite right. I put my fingers against my wrist and there's like this sound in my veins and I know my heart has stopped pumping. I'm alive and dead.

I always suspected you were a zombie.

I'm being serious. I watch people to see if they react differently to me but they don't. I go home and have some supper and go to bed and then

187

repeat it all over all again.

Groundhog Day.

Story of my frigging life, Lucas. And sometimes I dream my heart has actually moved. It's located in my head or knee. One time I carried it around all day like a bairn in a pushchair. Folk stopping me in the street, gushing about how beautiful it is. Ugh.

They are silent. All Sheila can focus on is the sound of the baby's mewls.

She says, I'm a bad person.

What's going on with you?

The baby's keening cranks up a notch and Sheila watches the young father pass the baby to the mother and the mother undoes her top and places her nipple in the baby's mouth and the father watches his partner watching the baby with so much love and contentment and—

Sheila says, I don't know where to begin.

They stop beside a way-sign on the Cleveland Way to drink some tepid water from a bottle. In the field beside them, a rook is devouring a fresh cow pat. In the distance the headland of Scarborough is veiled in a citrus haze.

Lucas says, Can you hear that?

They step closer to the cliff edge. A small crowd has gathered on the beach below. They follow the path down.

Children are touching the beached whale's tongue and teeth and jaw. A Rottweiler is licking at a fin.

Lucas says, It's a young minke.

Check out David Attenborough.

They'll be here soon.

Who?

Experts. Staff from the Sea Life Centre. Can't've been here long. Tide's just gone out. Get trapped in the shallows. Saw one here a few months back. Saw them dispose of it. Tractor with a digger. Dug a hole, buried it. Chopped it up first with the fork things on the front. Guts exploded with the gasses inside. Bleurgh.

You think they'd take it away.

And do what?

Tests.

Imagine how much she weighs.

She?

Looks like a young girl. Don't you think?

Do whales have belly buttons?

Random.

Thanks.

You're the very definition of weird-osity You're weird-ocious.

They move closer. The animal is covered in scratch marks, deep lines etched into its skin.

It's beautiful, she says.

She steps between a couple of young men taking photos on their mobile phones. Instagrams of death. She reaches out, touches the whale with her fingertips and then both hands. She has the urge to hug it.

It feels like a tomato, she says.

No. A hotdog.

Memory foam.

Patent leather!

It stinks, she says.

It really fucking hums.

They step away from the crowd and move down to the tideline. At the water's edge, a shadow passes over the beach, like the shadow of a giant bird. She eyes the clouds for a moment. A canoeist appears to her right, skimming over the bounds of the water with a hollow tapping sound, struggling against the current, it seems.

She stares out across the shelf of the North Sea, thinking about her father on his ships and frigates. How it felt like he was always avoiding them. Dad, up early, bed made, small tiny disciplines and didn't they know it—the kind of man who ironed his underwear and handkerchiefs and pillowcases. He was a pain in the arse sometimes, and sometimes it was a relief when he went back to sea. Owt but the constant nag-nag-nag. But deep down it hurt. Christmas mornings talking to him on his frigate, he always sounded so stressed and monotone and the satellite signal kept disintegrating. It was great to hear his voice and that things were OK but after they hung up Mam always looked glassy-eyed and downcast and went to her room to cry. He hated being retired. He was dead within six months. These thoughts about him—it's as if they have been in a box all these years. She wonders what else is in there.

Sheila turns. Lucas is crouched on the sand examining a dead bird. Again, she thinks about the last time she saw Jake in her flat. Her last words to him: Don't hurt anyone else. But did she mean: Don't hurt me.

That wasn't a goodbye. It was a badbye.

She closes her eyes. Listens to the lop of waves.

Jake, head bowed in her hallway, all he needed was a hug and a place to stay for the night. The distant thump of the front door. Gone. She didn't even go to the window to watch him walk away.

And I cannot let you in.

What kind of a woman falls for a grieving man?

Badbye.

She opens her eyes again. Downy clouds pursue each other over the pewter-coloured sea.

She still loves Scarborough with its Georgian crescents and tacky magic shops, gobby Geordies and fish and chip parlours, and she will always feel the tug of the North Sea, but the pull of Nethergill is so much stronger now.

She says to Lucas, I want to go home.

I know. Is there owt more depressing than a beached whale?

No, she says. I mean home home.

JULY

Bear opens the door with Clem in his arms.

Welcome back to the Hotel California.

Babysitting, are we?

A slow half-grin. If only.

The bairn is quiet, sucking at his fist.

Sheila dumps her cases in the hallway. She goes to kiss Clem but he pulls his head away with a squawk.

Bear says, Karen's moved in.

Eh?

Just racked up on Sunday.

She dumped him?

Not sure.

Why didn't you tell me?

Was worried you wouldn't come.

You knew I was coming?

Don't you remember calling me one night?

No.

Bouncing Clem up and down on his hip, he says, You were pretty hammered like. Said some nice things though.

Sake. She here?

Out.

They move through into the living room. The dogs start barking and Bear shouts at them. Sheila eyes the state of the place.

So where am I meant to kip?

With me.

Oh. I see.

It's not like that.

Then why you grinning like a Cheshire cat?

I'm not.

Shut up!

The dogs cower. Clem starts to laugh—a laugh creepily grown-up and sarcastic.

She says, Me and you and Karen and Clem and the frigging dogs? Jesus wept. I'll have another cardiac. I'm not kidding.

You're in fine fettle.

I'll stay with Mam until all of this is sorted.

Whatever.

Oh, put the Spawn of Satan down and give us a bloody hug.

Later. Sheila leaves the funeral home, crosses the street and climbs into Bear's battered Frontera, placing the box of cremains on the dashboard.

So, there he is, Bear says.

Sheila nods. There he is.

They continue to stare at it.

Howay, Bear says, and touches her face.

It's weird. It felt weird when my dad died and it feels weird now. Not the fact that he's dead but that he's in a tiny box. Won't be a grave to go and visit.

Bear returns his hands to the steering wheel.

She says, Why didn't he want to be buried near Edith or William? I know he was anti-God and all that, but no service? And why did he want to be scattered on top of Penhill?

Maybe he liked the idea of being—I don't know. Place must've meant summat. He never say owt?

Sheila pulls the box onto her lap.

He says, You loved him, didn't you?

She chews her bottom lip. Thought I'd be distraught but I just feel so… Let's go. I can't think about this anymore.

Back at Bear's, she puts Jake on the sideboard and sits down on the settee. Bear comes through with a large glass of vodka and ice. She cups it in her hands and stares down into it. The dogs whinge and yap in the other room.

You feel any better? he says.

A sip. A shrug. A sip.

He sits beside her. Sorry if I was a bit gruff before.

She hands him the glass and gets up and opens the box of cremains. The white-grey ashes feel grainy between her fingers.

This town, she says. You love the fact it's like Trumpton, don't you? Everyone knowing everyone else's business. The sugary sarcasm. The criticism. But you realise, soon as folk find out Jake left me the cottage. I keep getting snooty looks as it is. Inheriting the land. Just makes me feel so flaming…

What?

Guilty.

She still hasn't told Mam or Bear about the money Jake left her. It doesn't feel real. Doesn't feel right.

I think I'm going to sell it. With everything that's happened, you know? Last thing I want to do is disrespect the community. More than they have been, I mean.

She returns the ashes to the box.

I'm off for a walk.

The sky is anti-freeze blue, pearling the charred remains of Dove Cottage. The top half of the building has collapsed. Jake's bedroom is in the kitchen and William's is in the living room. She'd peeked into William's room a couple of times when she was visiting Jake. Furniture like skeletons. Rocks and fossils and hunting gear. Pages torn from magazines on the walls. Model aeroplanes hanging on threads candy-flossed with dust. Picturing William in bed making sound effects, the beam of his torchlight scanning the skies for enemy craft.

She steps over the tape. The heat has even softened the window glass. The remaining walls aslant, crumbling in the weather. Mould growing among the ash, soot, exposed rebars, tumbled masonry. You can even see parts of the foundations—they look bright pink. Outside, through a gap in what should have been the dining room wall, the lush rowan stands untouched, completely out of place among the scorch and tilt.

Such a mess you've made.

She'll Google companies when she gets home. Get it cleared. Nowt left but the foundations, land. The start of something. But what?

Beside her feet an object shimmers. She picks it up, half-expecting her fingers to get burnt. A jar of cinnamon hand cream.

Again, she hears Jake's voice in her head. She turns around, fully expecting him to find him here.

Fucking arsehole, she says.

Later. Staring at the box of cremains, she realises it doesn't feel like Jake anymore—not the forgetting of what's inside but the way it becomes just a box. Bits of others, communal ash. As if he has obliterated himself. But the guilt has lasted—the guilt is right here in this room, Sheila carrying it around inside her like an extra organ.

Jake?

She holds her breath.

Again: Jake?

She smiles. I miss you, she says. Think about you every day. But I hate you for what you did. Sometimes I blame myself for leaving Nettlebed. If I hadn't been so selfish and moved away then maybe…or was it summat that was always going to happen? Was that your plan all along? Couldn't you rise above it? This man-thing. Need for violence. Because anger gets shit done.

Sheila?

She turns. Bear is in the doorway, face dark.

Who you talking to?

No one. Her heart is an egg hatching.

She says, Mam said summat to me earlier. That William wasn't Jake's. That he was Charles Monroe's?

Bear steps closer. That's what folk reckon.

Why didn't you say owt?

You've enough on your plate.

But I just can't put the two facts together. Jake, the man I knew, keeping it a secret all of his life. And the fact that Edith cheated on him. Way he idealised her.

Bear, half-smiling: Charles obviously fancied a bit of rough.

Rough? You're joking, aren't you? She was stunning.

I meant working class.

He opens his arms but she places a hand on his chest and steps back.

She says, William's half-brother killed Jake.

She says, Jake killed his son's real father. And when he placed his hands around Charles' neck, he—

What?

With something burning behind her skin, she raises both hands and slowly brings them together. Grief and anger, she says, and Bear whispers, Love, and she sees herself reflected in his large green eyes.

AUGUST

She takes her handbag from the cloakroom and exits the Unit. It has been one of those shifts. Usually, once her client drops off to sleep, she can have a sneaky nap, but he was suffering with his new meds and they had to watch TV while she tried to soothe him. He has an annoying tic of making loud sound effects and repeating sound bites and TV catchphrases:

> *We buy any car dot com.*
> *Finger lickin' good.*
> *Because I'm worth it.*
> *It's a bit of an animal.*
> *You know when you've been Tango'd!*

On a loop all night until he fell into a twitching sleep just before dawn, ten minutes before her colleague appeared for the handover.

Typical.

It is the beginning of her three days off and she is praying Karen has taken Clem out so she can get some kip.

She unbuttons her sexless uniform and rubs her stomach. She's gasping for a cigarette.

She showers and shaves her legs and strains to do the top button on her shorts. When was the last time she'd worn them? She breathes in, straightens her back and manages to get the button through the hole but it bites into her stomach and then pops onto the floor. She climbs onto the scales for the third time today.

Bear removes his shirt and sits beside her on the bench. She eyes him from behind her mirrored shades. She forgot how hairy and tattooed and utterly massive he is. The light reflecting off his tanned skin makes him look like he is cast from bronze—a biker Buddha.

He says, Karen tells me you've got her a job at the Co-op? His smile breaks into laughter.

Should have heard the language.

How'd we manage to raise a bairn so idle?

She shrugs. Guess I was as daft at her age.

She recounts her teenage years for him, knocking around with kids on the estate in the 1970s. He's heard it all before but she just enjoys telling him. Bottles of cider from a hatch in the Black Swan. Sitting around the Hullah's house watching dirty videos. Shoplifting from Molly Auton's and Fine Fare. Stealing a sofa from the back of Darwin's Saleroom and carrying it down to the field near the beck, to the secret shed where she first smoked and first fucked. Her light-fingered cousin, Albert, on his old butcher's bike, fag in his gob, sent to borstal. Finding Mark fiddling with his sister down by the sewerage works. Sherriff with his little junk shop, a run-down shed full of second-hand tat, keeping warm by the single bar of his electric fire. Watching ambulances wheeling dead bodies out the back of Mowbray Grange. Dressing up as old folks at Halloween. Christmases drunk, carol singing to get cash for more cider.

She says, Mind you, I was never work-shy. Always got to the farm early. Grafted twice as hard as the boys. Don't know where Karen gets it from.

Plays us off each other.

Nah, she says. It's because you're a pussy and I'm a dick.

Making his way through a six-pack and sweating in the sun with his long nicotine-coloured hair sticking to his shoulders. He looks peaceful, sublime.

She first fell in love with him because he grew up on two wheels and if he died on the road, he'd die happy. There was something in that statement she found both unfathomable and deeply erotic. Imaging the rough texture of his life back then, the raffish Bear living by the seat of his pants, riding out for days with the Banshees. And even though he was a salty mountain man renowned for being handy with his fists, he was soft and gentle and never not once raised his voice to her. Which was basically the complete opposite of her first husband, Steve. By comparison, her life with Bear was the sugar-tit life and he filled in the chunks Steve had torn from her. But after a few years she began to wish he was a little bit more wilful and grew frustrated with him. Nowt about that made any sense.

Steve, she says.

What about him?

She's never really opened up to Bear about Steve because she's always been worried about what he'd do. Because she knows men are insecure and unpredictable. But she has no idea where Steve is anymore. Down in Leeds, was the last she heard. Good riddance.

She opens her mouth, pauses. I've been thinking about Jake, she says. About what you told me. That Charles fathered Jake's son. Last night I remembered this conversation I had with him about Steve. The fact Steve was infertile.

199

Bear is breathing hard.

And I remember Jake gave me this queer look. I thought it was just, you know, that he's like you, protective and that. But it wasn't, was it? It was summat else.

She says, I Googled it this morning. Cuckoldry. Apparently, there are loads of men raising kids that aren't theirs. Statistically. Summat like one in fifty men. I know. I think they make this shit up.

She says, And then there's all this stuff about the mating habits of stags. The dominant stag kicks the other stags' arses and then shags their wives. He has a what's-it-called? Harem. Then the stag wees on himself and the smell of his piss makes all of the females ovulate. I know. And then he humps them all! And as I was reading this I kept thinking: But what's it called if you know the bairn isn't yours? Is there even a name for that?

She says, Imagine Edith telling him she was pregnant. Not knowing how to react. Then gradually falling in love with the lad. Taking strength from him. From his love. The forgetting. It must be like a box you never open.

I don't know what you're saying.

Delusion.

The scud of her heart. The fracture of Bear's breath.

Bear says, Charles put his thumb in Jake's pot and sired a spare and Jake raised it as his own. That's all there is to it. Jake wasn't one of those wankers in the pub going on about how hard they are. He was the real deal. The toughest fucker I've ever met and he raised that bairn as his own and elected to keep his gob shut.

He adds, Jake was the stag. Not Charles.

Sheila nods, unsure, recalling Edith the frowner, the tutter, the puckerer of lips and sucker of teeth. The constant sigher. An old battle axe to avoid.

She says, But why would Jake do it?

Bear says, Whatever the reason, most men wouldn't. End of. What's the saying? Any dickhead can sire a bairn but it takes a man to raise a child. Besides, things were different back then.

Were they?

Aye.

But were they?

She eyes Bear's left hand, the mark where his wedding ring has cinched his doughy finger. Why does he take it off when she's around?

Those hands. Those large powerful hands that have brought her so much pleasure over the years, making things and shaping things and holding her close. Keeping her safe. She pushes the thought from her head and casts her eyes around the scrappy garden. The grass needs doing.

He crushes his beer can and opens another.

She recalls the months leading up to their separation. He took voluntary redundancy from the carpet company but he was too proud to claim benefits and so they struggled on one wage for a while. He talked about joining the railways (the training period was too long, he said) and then becoming a bus driver (he couldn't imagine putting up with the shit drivers on the road) and then a taxi driver (same reason). He began sleeping late and stopped dressing during the day. Stopped seeing the old gang members. Barely muttered more than one syllable or registered Sheila or Karen's presence in the house. Stuck in his armchair like he was stuck in his self-pity.

Sheila can picture him now, the happy-go-lucky gentle giant who quickly became the silent layabout, glassy-eyed and downcast, saying, I just don't know what to do. Sheila cutting back with, Less of the boo-hoo talk, Bear. Something'll come along. You've got to put yourself out there. But once he'd spent all of their savings he just disappeared further into himself. So, she kicked his woe-is-me arse out. But it wasn't meant to be permanent. He just never came home again.

There are another two or three hours of yolk yellow sunlight left before it sinks behind the trees. He leans back and digs a hand into his crotch and realigns himself with the universe. Her eyes are drawn, again, to the bulging buttons of his fly. He grins at her with his whole body. She swallows and reaches for her drink. The way his thumb rubs the sweat beaded around the can. The way he looks her in the eye while doing it—she feels her nipples crease against her bra.

She reapplies her lip-gloss. When's Karen back?

Later on.

Bear's leg is warm and bristly against hers. She returns the pressure and then reaches under the table and squeezes his thigh, and with the rush of need and desperation in her eyes, she says, Get your arse up them stairs.

He holds her in a vice-like clinch, his weight and warmth all around her, his bullish chest and arms and legs solid like tree limbs, breath hot and beery in her face.

He says, This all right?

She peers up into his face and for some reason she can't tell him she loves him. She reaches between his legs as he kisses her breasts.

Jesus, she says.

Are you OK?

Stop talking.

His tongue is wrapping around hers and something splits apart inside her. The blood-whirl of lust in her veins as he kisses her lip-gloss away.

They make love for the first time in four years. He fucks like he eats, messy and with a lot of noise. He's always known how to make her come but this time it feels like a betrayal because she is thinking about Jake, the rough texture and low burr of his voice, like a gnarled old tree trunk, the old-timer Dales accent, sentences abrupt and halting, an accent that could chop kindling, a woodman's axe straight into her soul.

She jolts awake. Rain glances off the panes. Bear rattles beside her. The digital clock says 19:41. Evening light seeps through the window. With

202

his arm folded over his eyes, he looks like a big hairy child. She feels the tug of the invisible line attaching them both. She lifts his hand and places it onto her face. The smell of all that he is.

She wakes him. He looks dazed.

She says, I think I know what to do.

What?

Jake's cottage, she says. The land.

The next morning, Karen is sitting at the table eating a bowl of cereal and pretending to read the free newspaper—as if she ever reads the newspaper. She is dressed smartly for her first day at the Co-op.

Sheila stands behind her and touches her hair. You could do with a trim.

Karen tuts and moves her head free. Sheila sighs and goes over to the sink and rinses a few cups. They are silent for a moment, listening to Clem trashing his playpen in the front room, growling like a bear cub.

Finally, Karen looks up at Sheila and asks, What?

Don't start acting up today.

Karen blinks a couple of times.

Do you hear me?

I feel like I'm being punished.

Don't talk daft. Standing on your own two feet? It's hardly a punishment. Just wait till you've got your first pay-cheque. Bit of money in your back pocket.

Karen casts her eyes toward the ceiling, sighs.

Sheila nods to herself, satisfied she's said the right thing, and then rummages through her workbag.

From behind her, Karen mutters: I was fine on benefits.

Sheila straightens but waits a moment before turning around. Are you really my flesh and blood? I swear they swapped you in the maternity ward.

Karen is silent. Sheila glares at her while playing with her house keys.

And don't be bringing Mike round here again. You hear me? I don't want to go for a pee in the middle of the night again and find *him* in the bathroom having a dump.

That shut Karen up. But Sheila wasn't quite finished yet.

Here's me skivvying away all the hours god sends and you're sat on your fat arse watching Judge Rinder. It's not on. Girl your age, with a bairn and all, you should be out grafting. Don't you *dare* screw this job up. You hear me? I'll pick Clem up from nursery on my way back from work, but you come straight back after your shift's finished. Straight. Back. Don't go gallivanting off.

OK, woman. I hear you.

Later. Sheila has bathed Clem and is just settling him down when, unusually, he falls straight to sleep. She heads downstairs to find Karen has come back from work and is watching TV, making her way through a bag of Maltesers. She looks knackered. Good.

Hope you paid for them? Sheila says.

Whatever.

What's up with you?

I'm fagged out.

Bit of graft. Must be a shock to your system?

Mam. A catch to her voice.

What?

Finally, Karen's eyes pull from the screen.

Mam—

Sheila folds her arms.

Karen bursts into tears. I'm late.

You can cut that shit out. You certain?

Done three tests.

Is it Mike's?

Course it's fucking Mike's.

How late are you?

Karen shrugs. Sheila tuts, her stare turning inwards. Did she not hammer it home often enough? Stick one on. Don't get tied down. A young woman with kids to different dads, men think you'll get on your back for anyone.

You're an idiot, Sheila says.

Pot kettle.

Later. She shoves Karen's feet to one side and sits beside her on the bed.

I'm sorry, Karen says.

It's what happens next that matters.

I found out last week...he's already got a bairn.

Jesus.

A daughter he has nowt to do with.

Please tell me you haven't told him you're pregnant?

No.

Good. Then the useless twat doesn't need to know.

Know what?

That you're getting rid of it.

Sounds from the street coming through the open window—children's laughter, shouting.

Congested with tears and snot, Karen's sinuses squeak.

Then Sheila wonders why it is so easy for her to insist—in a heartbeat—that Karen has an abortion. Is it because she knows she will only end up having to look after it? Is she really that selfish? Or is it something else?

Northallerton Coroner's Court. The main road is busy with traffic, glints off chrome and glass, the summer sun assaulting her senses. She looks at Bear, he looks at her. She hasn't been called to give evidence but she was told her statement will probably be used, perhaps even read out in part. It's entirely up to you if you want to attend.

They sit at the back with a clear view of the coroner—a tanned middle-aged woman sitting on a red leather chair behind an antique table. Mounted on the wall above her: a coat of arms and a framed picture of a young Queen Elizabeth. She is reading rapidly from her notes, clipped tones, emotionless, her voice slightly amplified by a microphone hanging from the ceiling.

—stating on the thirtieth of April this year a police officer from the North Yorkshire Constabulary reported Jake's death. We had been told that he had been found deceased at Aysgarth Falls by two members of the public.

Sheila sits with her spine very straight and her sweaty hands resting on her thighs. Her mouth is dry. There are bottles of water and stacks of paper cups on a nearby table but she doesn't want to get up and draw attention to herself because a couple of reporters are sitting just to her left.

Bear removes his jacket, bundles it in his lap.

Let me just explain what we need to do today. I'm required by law to carry out an investigation into the cause of somebody's death. The inquest itself is a means of bringing together the various threads of the investigation and making connections...

Sheila leans towards Bear and whispers, I don't think I can do this.

He frowns at her.

The legal questions I'm obliged to answer, if I'm able to, are laid down in legislation. At the end of the inquest once I've listened to the evidence I'm to determine the answers to a number of limited but nevertheless vitally important questions. They are: who the deceased was, where, when, how...

Bear is still looking at her.

In the silences between the coroner's statements you can hear the sound of people moving about in the offices upstairs.

But this is a fact-finding inquiry. I'm not here to determine any questions of liability or apportion any blame...

To Sheila's right is a window. Beyond the window, a man in the car park is tipping rubbish into a wheelie bin.

The police officer asked one of her colleagues to carry out a toxicology analysis, a Mr Baume, resident toxicologist at James Cook University Hospital. He found that there was some ethanol, some alcohol present in Jake's blood, at the level of 159 milligrams per decilitre, so not an excessive amount...

She says, The rate of all metabolic processes slows down, leading to loss of judgement, apathy, disorientation, and lethargy...

She says, Scavengers also affected the rate of decomposition...

Sheila whispers, Did she say birds?

What I'm going to do now is call the police officer forward to give her evidence and then I'll give you an opportunity to ask her any questions you may have. So, if I could ask you to come into the witness box.

Heads turn as the young female officer climbs into the box to take the oath.

Sheila imagines the mother and son who found Jake's body, waiting for the police to arrive, wildlife making noises in the dark around them, the crackle of the officer's radio, distant sound of police quad bikes and scramblers. How scared they must have been. How totally freaked out.

Nothing of significance. But, yes, there were obvious injuries from wildlife.

What was your interpretation, then, of what had happened?

Sheila stares at the back of the chair in front of her. She can't focus. She is aware of Bear beside her and of the bright ceiling lights and the sound of the young officer's voice, but as something peripheral. Then Sheila is watching Sheila get to her feet and walk out of the room, down the corridor, through the waiting room and out into the raging summer sun. Pausing beside the main road, watching traffic whirring by.

Bear takes her hand in his, threading fingers.

Later that day, steering north across Jackdaw Moor, the taxi's windscreen striped by long afternoon shadows, she makes small talk with the driver but really, she just wants to sit here and be quiet and watch the land scroll by. She didn't want Bear to drive her here. Didn't want to have to explain or lie again. The driver twists the dial on the stereo and eyes Sheila in the rear-view. They cross a humpbacked bridge and then a cattle grid onto the high moor. There are no walls up here and often it feels like they might slide off the road into a deep ghyll.

The taxi driver says, Hear the inquest was this morning.

Trumpton.

Sorry?

Just up here'll do.

You sure?

Come get me in a couple of hours.

The man pulls into a small car park, shuts off the engine and turns to face her.

You sure you're OK?

She sits in the shade of an outcrop, removes her sunglasses and scans the marl lake below. There isn't a cloud in the sky and yet the lake looks black, solid. She leans her head against the rock, eyeing the distant clinch of hillsides, recalling the light caught in the hairs along Jake's muscular forearms, the look on his face when she told him she was leaving. The last thing she expected him to do was to grab her arms and start dancing and singing.

So much had been staring her right in the face. Why else would he come to her in his hour of need? Why else would she turn him away?

She heads back down the dale towards the woodland beside the beck.

From daylight to shadow, the temperature a few degrees cooler amid the trees, her skin goose-fleshing, she unties her cardigan from her waist and notices a fallen tree in a clearing. She pulls on her cardigan and sits on the trunk. For a long time, she watches the soft slow movement of the sun infiltrating the canopy, dapples and spotlights rippling the woodland floor, bringing the smell of gorse and broom. Something creeps inside her, a feeling that something has gone, that some kernel of the trauma has, perhaps, left her body.

Or has it just changed into something else?

Two days later, Sheila and Bear are in the conservatory, drinking tea and snacking on cheese and biscuits. It gets too hot as the sun edges around the side of the house and so they move into the garden and sit in the shade of the wall. Bear opens a box of cider and they drink into the afternoon. The conversation turns to what they are going to do about Karen and their living arrangements.

Don't fret, she says. I've got it covered.

Since when?

I says to her, If you can keep the job down for a year, I'll help you out with a mortgage on a flat.

And you were going to tell me this when?

You should be chuffed.

He shakes his head. So, me and you?

What about it?

He shrugs.

No rush is there? Not like we're doing it for the first time.

He nods, says, I know you made a pal in Lucas and he's welcome over here any time. But I don't want you going back to Scarborough.

(Somehow, Bear knows about her sleeping with Dai.)

She frowns a question mark at him and says, I don't intend going back. But don't you start telling me what I can and cannot do. OK?

Sorry.

Well think on.

SEPTEMBER

Gunning the Frontera along the uneven surface of the road, tools rattling on the backseat, Bear rubs his eyes and then turns off the music, staring hard into the beams of the headlights. The land beyond is ink-dark and yet the horizon is diesel blue. He sighs thinking about the drive over to Carlisle that afternoon to pick up the new bit of kit to attach a Velorex to a Triumph Bonneville. All he wants is to get home and see Sheila. The late summer heat makes him unctuous and snarky. He peels his plaid shirt from his clammy back, turns off the aircon and opens the window.

Pete, the whipper-in, one of Lip Monroe's men. He came to see Bear last night. Said he knows where Lip has been hiding. Lad's a dim-bulb but he isn't a liar. And Bear's thoughts turned to the inquest and the litany of injuries Jake sustained at Lip's hands.

Back at home he finds the house empty. He feeds the dogs and rolls a joint and steps into the dark field behind the house. Beyond the oak trees he can just make out the sails of the farmer's small wind turbine on the nearby hillside. He picks tobacco from the tip of his tongue and tilts his head back, the northern skies so deep and starless, and a sudden breeze makes him close his eyes.

He thinks about Edith's funeral a couple of years ago. The poor turn-out.

Thumbing the wedding ring on his finger, his thoughts bend between what he knows he should do and what he can get away with. A stirring inside him that can't be staved. He smokes the joint to the roach, flicks it into the grass and heads back into the house.

Across the fields to the fast-running beck, she sits beneath the shade of the weeping willow tree, its branches toying with the water as if it is admiring its own reflection. The afternoon is sticky-warm and drowsy. Insects buzz around the bushes. Bees loop through the air, fat and drunk. Sunlight spangles the water.

She has designed every detail in her head. Twenty-five 75-foot beds. Two large polytunnels. High rotation, high yield per square foot. Replacing Jake's hurt and grief and violence with love and nourishment and dirt. A community, therapeutic garden. Generosity. Forgiveness. Lessen this second-hand shame. The solicitor has agreed to become one of the trustees and help with all of the tax and legal stuff. She is going to ask Bear to be the other trustee. Because what else can you do with all this anger and let-down other than try and turn it into something pure, and there's nowt as pure as your fingers in the dirt.

On the bank beside the willow is a crab apple tree with its lime green fruits, leaves turning black and matt with mould. Someone planted that, she thinks. Next to the bench with its inscription about how so-and-so liked to sit here.

Choose a name and structure for the charity, the solicitor said. Create a governing document. But she doesn't want the name to have owt to do with Jake. Or the Monroes. Something new, positive. Let the community choose.

She watches the water. Flash of scales beneath the murk. A couple of brown-white signets float through bulrushes on the opposite bank. Above her, black specs of swallows flying low, catching insects on the wing.

High price-per-pound, mature or harvest in sixty days or less. Lettuce. Radishes. Turnips. Leafy greens. Include local heritage varieties. Take pests and germination problems into account and calculate the average. Hire volunteers to help with the maintenance and harvesting. Landscaping, digging, picking. Invest the pre-tax profits back into the community.

A squirrel dashes through the branches above, rustling the fine yellow leaves of the willow tree. It barks, flicks its tail. She raises a hand, makes a finger-and-thumb pistol, pulls the trigger. Bang!

A betrayal. That's what it was. A fucking betrayal.

Yes, the new me. The sweary me.

Your fault, you fucking old twat.

Three weeks ago, a specialist company cleared what was left of the cottage. A structural engineer examined the foundations. Preserve as much of them as possible, she said. Last week he phoned to say a quarter of the foundation was full of spalls and wasn't reusable. The fire had been so intense parts of the concrete had returned to lime.

Get rid of the damaged section, she said. The part that can be repaired will be used for an accessible toilet and a shelter.

She plans to build a sensory garden. Sort out the path widths. Use textured surfaces. Build some places to sit, rest. Maybe get a sculptor on board. Set up some courses. Show people how to grow and plant out and harvest. Get school kids up there, get their nubbins in the dirt. But she was going to need help setting up the whole enterprise. She planned to have an open day—a tea tent, stalls of home baking and plant sales. Get someone in to give a talk. A horticulturalist. People can bring picnics. Propagation and pruning, watering and digging. A Horticultural Task Force! Buy a van to deliver produce. A stall at the indoor market. Planting hedges and compost making. And let the community choose a name. Let the guest speaker pick one out of a hat. Alan fucking Titchmarsh! Return the land to the commoners. Plant a small orchard. Make cider and perry! Oo-arrr!

She moves down to the water's edge and steps into the beck. The water is deep and black and chilly enough to make her gasp. Gliding silently as a swan she swims upstream and then twists onto her back and allows the tug of the current to pull her downstream. Moving her arms through the water she feels like she is flying through the scroll of clouds above, and as she smiles her crooked-teeth smile, dapples of light make her apple-green eyes sparkle, the freckles on her skin joining hands.

She pulls the view into her, feeling it at the centre of her being.

Three nights later. Driving into the night across Jackdaw Moor, four of them in the car: Bear, Tank, Boulder and Lip Monroe, the air full of cigarette smoke and adrenaline. Behind the car, the rumble of three motorbikes. Lip has been hiding at an old girlfriend's house, so close to home all this time, recovering. Hands on the wheel, Bear gives a half wave out of the windscreen as if greeting what is about to befall Lip. He takes a deep breath and starts to sing.

I took my fowlpiece in my hand,
Resolved to fire if Tom should stand.
He heard a noise and turned him round,
I fired and brought him to the ground,
My hand gave him the deep death wound...

Lip watches the dark moorland passing by outside, as if only vaguely aware of the proceedings.

Soon they pull into the car park at the crest of the moor.

A lone, wind-bent tree.

Bear switches off the engine, reaches for his tobacco and papers.

Lip's breathing fills the car.

Bear brings the hand-rolled fag to his lips like a mouth organ, sealing it with a swipe of his tongue. He lights it and turns around in his seat, exhaling a smoky smile.

The flicker of Lip's scar-crossed eyebrows.

Bear says, It's time for you to get out.

Listen. He's coming up the stairs. Swish of socks across the landing. His heavy breathing in the room. She pictures him staring at the back of her head with his Listerine green eyes. Dull clunk of a glass on the sideboard. Clink of his wedding ring. A drawer being slid open. What's he doing? Dip of the mattress behind her.

He whispers, You awake?

No. Come to bed. Her voice has that radio tone to it, like she's been rehearsing the line. She wants to tell him: I don't like the thoughts in my head. And: I want to get out of here. Travel. Escape. See the world. Come with me. Something to avert the truth of what's happening. Bring them closer. Erase what Jake did and how it has made her feel. What it has brought to the surface of things.

Bear runs his hand across her hair. The smell of tobacco on his fingers and something else. Coins. Now she knows.

There's summat I need to tell you, he says.

No, she says. I don't want to hear.

OCTOBER

Reclining on a deck chair in the shade of the rowan tree, music blasting through her headphones, she is transfixed by a ladybird scaling her leg, opening its shell to reveal its translucent brown wings. It takes flight, making her smile. A sudden movement startles her. She pulls off her headphones.

Shit the bed, she says. You proper scared me.

Bear passes her a bottle of ginger ale. She can smell something coming off him. Not sweat, something earthy.

She takes a swig. Where's your walking stick?

In the car. They feel OK today.

My dodgy ticker and your dodgy knees. What a pair.

Is Karen coming up?

Said so.

Won't hold my breath.

Eyeing the plots, Sheila is heartened to think how she will help breathe life back into this soil. Thinking about Jake and Edith's hands in this earth. The way Jake idealised her. Burying the truth all those years.

Bear sits beside her on the old oak chopping block and rubs his hairy, tattooed calves. The moor is filled with the scratch of insects, hiss of pippits. She gulps down the tepid ginger ale, stifling a belch.

Bear says, What's the plan?

See the sticks?

A-huh.

They're the corner points for the beds. We need to run brick lines around them all, about an inch from the ground. Help folk visualise the plots better.

I see.

You will. Then we dig out the inner portions.

Shouldn't we wait until the volunteers start?

We'll do just the one. Then they can see what needs to be done, eh.

Right.

She laughs. Need to stop getting ahead of myself. Realise I don't need to do this all on my own. It's not about me anymore.

When do the tunnels arrive?

Tuesday.

Need a hand?

No, apeth. Told you. Team of blokes are coming. Day's work they reckon. I'll come to supervise but that's it. Bring them some sandwiches and pop.

The plots, the tunnels, the new fences and faces—they'll be such a sharp contrast to the murky moors beyond that still look fagged out from last winter.

Noticing the box beside her feet, Bear says, What's that doing here?

Jake's ashes?

A-huh.

She picks up the box, shakes it. Thought he'd make good fertiliser.

You're joking?

Like putting a fingernail in soil and growing a whole new person.

What?

Nowt.

What about Penhill? His wishes and that?

She shrugs.

They didn't know it, but this was Jake's favourite time of year, the beginning of autumn—what Edith used to call the 'back end'. Perhaps, working this plot of land, they will start to read the landscape as Jake once had. Notice how the blackbirds come to attack the fruit on the rowan tree and all around them is a final burst of colour, not just from the changing leaves but from the seed heads and clutches of berries, hedgerows bursting with hips and haws, bryonies and sloes, attracting flies and wasps and all manner of birds that will shit the seeds out in a splatter of rainbow-white.

Jake would miss seeing his friends in the garden, the robins and toads and jays and magpies that come to dig holes and plant acorns. He often wondered if the clutch of house martins would return to the same nest under the eaves the following year. Wondered if Sheila would be living in Dove Cottage and marvel at them as he had.

The blowy afternoons of autumn, intimations of chill sweeping down over Jackdaw Moor, wind-blown leaves like strips of leather, the birds falling silent as they begin to moult, and between mole heaves, lace-worked with hoar-frost, spider threads, spangled with dewdrops, will be carpeting the plots.

It is the time of year when Jake's thoughts always returned to the back end of his childhood, walking to school across the meadows, moving his hands through the flower heads like some god mixing the firmament, cattle hock-deep in hawkbit and quaking grass, plough teams walking their daily acres, stooks of wheat propped in the fields, and the whump and crack of the baler was the summer-end beat of his heart. Because that's what he would miss the most—the seasons spinning like a revolving door, repeating into a future without him. Because what he saw in autumn was a new beginning.

Under the pale-grey sky Sheila and Bear pick up their spades and begin turning Jake into the dirt. Beside them, a knot of chaffinch squabble over berries in a briar.

Thank you, Vanessa Sutton, Peter Wright, Tom Georgeson, Emerson Mayes, Dr Will Loveday, Chris Leighton, Ron Crofts, Gaynor Dale, Emma Lannie, Esther Davis, Tracy Snowdon, Lorraine Daniels, The Yorkshire Garland Group, Chris Simms, Annie Clarkson, Chris Crouch, Mark Anderson, Steve Corn, Steve Jones, Ray Anderson, Paul Taylor, Sukey Fisher, Lucy Cooch, Aki Schilz, Karol Griffiths, Cat Donnelly, Kit Caless.

Thank you, Christian Cooke, Peter Mullan, Michelle Fairley, Sai Bennett, Elliott Tittensor, Si Bell, Sara and April at Mini Productions, and everyone who worked on and supported the short film, *Edith*.

Thank you, for everything, Scott Pack.